BORN TO PROTECT

ELITE FORCE SECURITY

CHRISTINA TETREAULT

Born To Protect, ©2018 by Christina Tetreault
Published by Christina Tetreault
Photographer: CJC Photography
Cover Model: Daniel Rengering
Cover Designer: Amanda Walker
Editing: Wordsmith Proofreading
Editing: Hot Tree Editing

ISBN: 978-1722957025

PROLOGUE

CONNOR STEPPED out of the elevator and noted the significant changes around him. *Someone's been busy up here.*

He'd worked for Elite Force Security for two and a half years and could count the number of times he'd visited the executive floor. He rarely had any reason to come up, and he preferred it that way. However, the director's assistant had called before Connor even reached home yesterday and told him to report to Eric Coleman's office first thing this morning. When the director summoned you, you didn't ask questions or refuse.

He approached the woman seated near the director's office. Well into her fifties, Winifred wasn't only the director's personal assistant but his wife as well and a former instructor at the FBI Academy. If the office gossip was anything to go by, the director and his assistant made all decisions pertaining to the firm together.

"I have a meeting with Mr. Coleman this morning," Connor said.

Winifred gave him an annoyed look and picked up the phone. On the few occasions he'd seen the woman, she'd worn a similar expression. Coworkers who had dealings with her said she always appeared either annoyed or mad. It was simply her natural state.

"Connor Anderson is here to see you," Winifred said. Rather than hang up, she pulled her legal pad closer and jotted down several notes. "Should I contact Senator Healey as well?" she asked as Connor continued to stand there. She added another note to her pad and hung up. "Mr. Coleman will see you now."

It was all he needed to hear. He was anxious to wrap up whatever the director needed him for, so he could head downstairs for the morning briefing.

A former FBI special agent in charge, Eric Coleman had taken over as the firm's director when his uncle stepped down. Unlike his wife, he never appeared anything but pleased to see you. Even when he intended to rip you a new one, he greeted you with a polite hello first—or at least that was what Connor had heard. To date, he'd never found himself on the man's bad side. He'd prefer to keep it that way.

Today Eric sat behind his desk. The flat-screen television mounted on one wall was tuned to a well-respected news outlet, but the volume had been muted. Various other computer screens were mounted on an opposite wall. At the moment, they all remained blank. Connor knew they were used for everything from watching hostage rescues unfold to conference calls with the director of the FBI and the Joint Chiefs of Staff, because although few knew it, Elite Force Security did much more than provide protection to anyone who could afford the firm's hefty prices.

"Connor, it's nice to see you again. Have a seat." The director gestured toward an empty chair. "I received a call yesterday from not only Curt Sherbrooke but also Jonathan Sherbrooke. Both wanted to let me know how pleased they were with the way you and your team handled the situation in Boston. And they wanted me to pass along how much they appreciated all you did to bring Reese home unharmed."

Between his time with the Marines and now with Elite Force,

he'd seen a lot of crap. Yet somehow people continued to amaze him when it came to the despicable things they did. And kidnapping your own child and holding her for ransom in an apartment filled with drugs and firearms fell well into the despicable category.

"I'm glad we were able to get her back to her aunt safely," Connor replied. As a member of Elite Force Security's Hostile Response Team, or HRT, he'd been the team leader for several hostage rescues. Before this one in Boston, none had ever involved a child. He prayed he never worked another one that did. Some things even he had a hard time handling.

Eric clasped his hands on his desk. "Both were disappointed when they heard you left the city the following morning. They wanted to thank you in person."

He would've left sooner if there had been a flight back to Virginia after they'd rescued the little girl from the apartment. In a past life, he'd loved Boston—all of New England actually. Now he only visited when he had no other choice.

"Curt wanted me to pass along his cell phone number. He said if you're ever in the area to give him a call."

It wasn't the first time he'd worked for the Sherbrooke family. The previous summer he'd been assigned to work as Allison Sherbrooke's bodyguard when a crazed stalker had been after her. He'd gone into the assignment with several preconceived ideas about her. For the most part, they'd turned out to be dead wrong. Judging by the messages the director delivered, many of the views Connor held in regard to the rest of the family were wrong too.

Eric passed him a sheet of paper. The name Curt Sherbrooke was written in the director's bold handwriting, and a phone number was listed under the name. Connor accepted the note, folded it, and stuck it into a pocket. Later it would find a new home in a wastebasket. He had no need of Curt Sherbrooke or the world he represented—a world he'd left behind more than fifteen years ago himself and had no desire to revisit.

"I thought you would've stayed in Boston longer. You have family there, don't you?" Eric inquired, clasping his hands again.

The guy knew damn well he had family there. The director did his homework before he allowed anyone to work for the firm. Others at Elite Force might not know his complete family history, but Eric and Ax Germaine, the head of HRT, did.

Connor nodded. "Yeah, my sister, Stephanie, and my stepbrother live in Boston. My stepsister is living near Hartford these days."

He enjoyed spending time with his younger sister, but he preferred to do it when she visited him. As for his stepbrother, he got along with the guy, but neither went out of their way to visit each other. And when it came to his stepsister, a woman who could teach the Wicked Witch a thing or two, he avoided her as much as possible. It had been at least a year, maybe more, since he last saw her.

The phone on Eric's desk rang, and he reached for it, putting an end to whatever question or comment he might throw at Connor next. "Excellent job again in Boston. Thank you."

Connor took the comment as permission to split.

While the top floor of the building housed the executive offices, the fourth floor was the home to Elite Force Security's cyber division as well as the Hostile Response Team. His meeting with the director over, Connor made his way down there.

When he walked into the team's meeting room, he found Ax seated at the head of the conference table. Those team members not out on assignment or vacation were there as well.

"Did that pretty waitress from Shooter's keep you in bed this morning?" Spike asked, giving him a knowing wink. "What's her name again? Sandy? Mandy?" He paused for a moment. "No, it's Candy, right?"

He'd gone out with Candy a handful of times, but hadn't seen or spoken to the waitress in months. He hadn't visited the pub in almost as long either, although it was one of his favorites. Before he could answer Spike, Keith spoke up.

"Nah, Coleman called him upstairs so he could kiss Connor's ass," Keith said from the opposite side of the table. "I heard the Sherbrookes called personally to tell Coleman how pleased they were with the work our dear Connor did up in Boston."

At the head of the table, Ax cleared his throat. "If you ladies are finished, we've got real work to do."

For the moment, joking went on hold, and Ax began the morning briefing. Later his teammates would go right back to busting his ass again. Not that Connor would have it any other way. The men and women he worked with were more than his coworkers— they were family.

Connor listened as Ax explained the details for the operation Ryan and Spike would lead in Mexico. The mission was to rescue a woman and her young daughter. The two had been forced to leave the country after the mom married a man she thought would be a great dad for her daughter back in January. Although an American citizen, the man turned out to be a terrorist sympathizer and an arms dealer who, for the past two years, had been supplying militants in Africa with both cash and weapons. Since both men spoke Spanish fluently, they were the logical choice to lead the team.

"Mad Dog and Connor, Shawn Butler requested you both for his family's vacation to France." Ax turned his attention their way.

Connor ground his teeth together and shot a look across the table at Madison Dempsey, better known around the team as Mad Dog. A former FBI SWAT team member, Mad Dog's expression told him she shared his enthusiasm for the assignment. A wealthy businessman from Australia, Shawn Butler regularly hired Elite Force to protect the family when they traveled overseas.

Usually when an individual or family hired the firm for similar jobs, the firm pulled from its supply of well-trained bodyguards and left the members of HRT to more important matters. When elite customers like the Butlers or Sherbrookes called, the bigwigs assigned members from the team instead.

The last time the higher-ups tapped HRT members to guard the family while on vacation, it had been after the Butlers received some death threats. Threats that had later proved to be a competitor's attempt to simply upset the guy before he went into business negotiations. Connor and Mad Dog had been given that assignment as well, and they'd spent a solid three weeks in England playing glorified babysitters. He'd rather be dodging bullets than babysitting Butler, his bitchy wife, and spoiled teenager daughter again. He knew Mad Dog shared his sentiments.

"I tried to get Coleman to send someone else, but he wouldn't budge. You'll meet the family in Sydney and then fly to Paris with them. Mary has booked your flights," Ax said. "First-class from here to Sydney, I'm told. Butler insisted. He wants you well rested and ready to go when you land."

Big surprise there. When someone with as much money as Shawn Butler made a request, it was honored. First-class, he could handle. And travel from Sydney to France would be even better. The Butlers didn't do commercial airlines. Oh no, they had their own private jet loaded with all the amenities to cart them around.

"How long will we be with them?" Mad Dog asked, reading his mind. If he had to travel with the family, he'd rather it be a short and sweet trip.

Ax checked his notes and grimaced. "Four weeks, but they've got the option to extend the contract if they want."

Damn, four weeks with that family would be like four years.

BECCA TOOK another sip of her tea and scrolled through the

news articles on her laptop. With no particular place to be until this afternoon, she planned to be lazy this morning.

"I didn't think I'd see you this morning before I left." Kassidy dropped her suitcase by the door and went straight for the coffee maker.

Becca didn't know exactly how much travel her stepsister had done before moving in with her, but in the past three months, it seemed like Kassidy had been gone more than she'd been home. Of course, part of that might be because she often spent her nights with whatever man she was currently sleeping with.

"How was your date last night?" Kassidy poured her coffee and then searched the fridge.

Becca couldn't contain an eye roll. "Short. I don't know what possessed Graham to suggest I go out with him."

It wasn't the first time her older brother set her up with one of his friends. Actually, except for Kassidy, all of her relatives, including her mom and dad, had tried setting her up with various friends or children of friends in the past. Last night's attempt had been the worst, though. Her brother and Nolan might get along well, but she had nothing in common with the man.

"You've met Graham's friend Nolan, right?" Becca asked.

Kassidy nodded as she set down her breakfast and coffee. "A few times. He didn't seem like my type, but he was nice enough. And he's gorgeous. Especially his eyes."

"He might be gorgeous, but he never stops talking about himself. Other than when I ordered dinner, I hardly got a word in all night."

"He did seem a little long-winded."

"Is that what you call it? I think he told me his whole life story between our appetizer and dinner." Becca took the last sip from her tea and went to make more. "Graham means well, but he needs to stop playing matchmaker. He stinks at it." She added a new tea bag and hot water to her mug. "Where are you off to this time?" She gestured toward the suitcase.

"New York. I feel the need for some shopping."

When she'd seen the suitcase, she'd automatically assumed her stepsister was traveling for work again. All of her recent travel had been. "If you'd told me, I would've taken time off and come with you. How long are you staying? I can probably meet you there next Friday. Maybe even late Thursday afternoon. My wardrobe could use some refreshing."

Growing up in Greenwich, Connecticut, she'd gone into New York City on a regular basis and made a point to visit whenever she could now. The last time she'd been there had been well over a year ago when she'd visited for New Year's Eve. There was nothing quite like New Year's Eve in Manhattan. There was also nothing like shopping in Manhattan.

Her stepsister paused with a spoonful of yogurt almost to her mouth. "I'm only there until Tuesday. I'm expected at a conference in Utah on Wednesday morning. I'll be there until Saturday, and then I'm off to Seattle for a meeting with one of the project leaders at the lab out there." Although Kassidy worked at Lafayette Laboratory's main facility in Annapolis, she often consulted with the researchers at the smaller ones.

Plenty of banked vacation time or not, there was no way she could make it to New York before Tuesday. "Next time you plan a short getaway, let me know. I'd love to come along, especially if you're going to New York." She'd taken a long weekend here and there but hadn't gone on a true vacation in longer than she cared to admit. "Are you going to see Mom and Robert?"

Becca's mom and her stepfather, Robert, divided their time between their estate in Connecticut and their home in Los Angeles. At the moment, they were in Connecticut and would be until December—or at least that was the plan the last time she spoke to her mom. However, Mom was known for making last-minute changes regardless of whether it was to the family's schedule or the house without consulting anyone. Becca suspected it was just one of the many reasons her parents had divorced when she was twelve. Thankfully, Mom's second husband didn't seem to mind the unexpected changes, no matter where in their life they popped up.

"When I talked to Deanna, I told her I'd stop in and see them," Kassidy answered.

She visualized her upcoming schedule, trying to determine when she might be able to jet off for a few days of shopping and perhaps a Broadway show or two. "Now that you mentioned New York, I want to go. What do you say we go up in three weeks? Ted will be gone then, so he won't need me around."

Senator Theodore Lynch was not only her boss but also a longtime family friend whom she'd grown up calling Uncle Ted. In three weeks, he had plans to escape to his vacation home on Martha's Vineyard to celebrate his wife's birthday. He'd even invited her to spend some time there with him and his family. As much as Becca loved the island and the Lynch family, she had no desire to spend the little free time she had with Ted, his wife, their children, and their many grandchildren.

"I'll let you know. There's a chance I'll be away."

The muffled sound of a ringing cell phone in the other room stopped Becca from commenting further.

"I'll be right back."

Becca watched Kassidy leave the room, then glanced back at the two silent cell phones on the kitchen table. One belonged to her and the other was her stepsister's. Did Kassidy now have a cell phone specifically for work? A lot of people these days carried two in an effort to keep their work and personal lives separate. Or was Kassidy again involved with a married man? When she had been seeing Steven, they'd both used cheap disposable phones to communicate. Not that it had stopped Steven's wife from finding out about the affair. The private investigator she'd hired had managed to get pictures of them together. Remarkably, despite the evidence of Steven's infidelity, the couple was still married—or at least they had been at Senator Lynch's holiday party last December. Since that was several months ago, it could have changed.

"It's none of my business," she said in a low voice. Kassidy could spend her time with whomever she wanted.

She dismissed the mystery of why Kassidy had two phones again and reached for her tea. Before she got the mug off the table, the theme song from *Gone with The Wind*, her mom's ringtone, filled the kitchen.

"Morning," she said.

"Hi, sweetie. I hope I'm not catching you at a bad time," her mom greeted. "I know you and Kassidy are probably too busy, but I wanted to invite you both, anyway. Sylvia is coming out with Ben and the girls this weekend before they fly to London."

Becca hadn't seen her stepsister Sylvia and her family since the previous Thanksgiving. If she'd had more notice, she would've arranged to go up for the weekend. She liked her stepsister and adored Sylvia's children. "Sorry, I can't…" She paused. Mom wanted to invite her and Kassidy? That didn't make sense. Kassidy already told Mom she'd visit this weekend. Deanna Buchanan might rearrange her calendar and living room every other day, but she never forgot or canceled when one of her children or stepchildren planned a visit. In her eyes, family came first.

"I wish I could, but there's no way I can come this weekend. But aren't you already expecting Kassidy? She's heading to New York today. She told me she already talked to you about visiting while she's there."

"I haven't spoken with Kassidy in at least a week. It might even be closer to three."

"Oh." Becca watched Kassidy enter the kitchen and grab the loaf of bread. "I must have misunderstood." Watching her stepsister, she considered her next words. "Say hi to everyone for me. And I'll try to get up for a visit soon."

At the counter, Kassidy made another slice of toast and sipped her coffee. After finishing her conversation, Becca set the phone down. Just what was going on with Kassidy? A few weeks ago, she'd caught Kassidy in a lie as well. She had no concrete evidence to back up the theory but, considering her conversation just now with Mom and the fact Kassidy had a second cell phone, she suspected her stepsister was again involved with a married man. She really didn't understand how Kassidy could be so intelligent, yet make such poor decisions when it came to dating. In fact, a poor decision involving the man she'd gotten involved with following Steven was why she was now living with Becca.

It's none of my business, Becca reminded herself again. Whatever secret Kassidy was keeping, whether it involved a man or not, wouldn't affect her life. Even as the words formed in her head, a seed of apprehension planted itself in her stomach.

ONE

ONE MONTH later

PULLING OPEN THE CAFÉ DOOR, Becca tried to ignore the sweat slipping down her back. Hot, sticky, and humid was the only way to describe today's weather. She'd merely walked from the medical building down the street to the café, and her blouse clung to her skin. Thank goodness she worked in an air-conditioned office. She couldn't imagine working outside on a day like this.

She passed the crowded tables and paused in front of the display cases. Blood work had been part of her yearly physical this morning, which meant she hadn't ingested anything but water since last night. Judging by the unladylike noises her stomach had started making while she dressed after her exam, her body was most displeased with her. Before she went into her blissfully cool office and the noises from her stomach scared away her coworkers, she needed to eat something.

The carrot cake muffin immediately caught her eye, and she joined the line of customers placing orders and looked over the various coffee options.

"What can I get for you this morning?" the employee behind the counter asked.

"Extra-large iced latte with nonfat milk and no sugar."

The woman grabbed a cup, scribbled notes on the side, and handed it off to another employee. "Anything else today?"

"Yes, a carrot cake muffin," Becca said. "Actually, make that a carrot cake muffin and a poppy seed muffin, please."

She'd cut all carbs from her diet in the spring, which had unfortunately included muffins and bagels—both of which she loved. Since she'd seen no huge health benefits from the little experiment, she'd decided last week to slowly reintroduce healthy carbs into her diet. Muffins certainly didn't fall into the healthy carbs category, but everyone needed to splurge from time to time. She'd enjoy one muffin now and save the other for tonight. Then she wouldn't have another for a few months.

With her order in hand, Becca scouted the café for a place to sit. Not long after taking her current position in Washington, she'd learned the hard way that eating and driving was a bad combination. Now she didn't even drink water while behind the wheel.

Although already ten o'clock on a Thursday morning, the place remained packed. She was about to give up on getting a seat and simply eat her snack in the car before she headed to the office when a college-aged man wearing a Georgetown University T-shirt left his spot at the counter near the windows.

Before anyone else could snag it, Becca made a beeline for the empty stool. She took a sip of her drink before she did anything else, the heavenly concoction of caffeine and cold milk hitting the spot, and sat. "Do you mind passing me a napkin?" she asked, glancing at her neighbor as she reached into the paper bag for a muffin. Her hand froze inside the bag when the man turned his head in her direction.

"Connor?" She searched for any sign the man recognized her. "Connor Anderson?" It had to be him. She often forgot where she left her house keys or cell phone, but she never forgot a face.

He shifted on the stool, his expression telling her everything. He recognized her but wasn't sure he wanted to acknowledge the fact. Finally, he nodded. "Becca André, right?"

His deep, sensual voice sent a ripple of awareness through her now, the same way it had when they were in high school. Becca nodded. "I haven't seen you since…" She caught herself before she brought up a topic Connor most likely would prefer to avoid. In his shoes, she would want to avoid it, anyway. "The summer after graduation. How are you?"

Actually, the last time she'd seen him had been at her best friend's end-of-summer party. She didn't remember every party she'd attended in high school, but she remembered that one well. It'd been a few days before everyone headed off to college. She and Connor had snuck into the pool house. They hadn't had sex, but they'd come darn close. If her older sister, Giselle, hadn't barged in and announced the FBI was at Connor's house, they probably would've.

The next day the news broke that Patrick Anderson, Connor's father, had been arrested. The following weekend Connor left for Harvard, and she'd headed down to Georgetown. Even though she'd tried calling him several times afterward, much to her disappointment, he hadn't returned any of the calls, and eventually, she gave up. As far as she knew, no one in their graduating class had seen him since then either, although she knew his mom and her second husband, Xavier Leonard, still lived in Greenwich. Actually, Mr. and Mrs. Leonard's home wasn't far from her mom and stepdad's house.

"Can't complain. You?"

Again Connor's voice washed over her, and Becca wished the café had the thermostat set a few degrees lower. "Good. Are you headed to work?" she asked.

She'd stopped in the café multiple times since it opened, and she'd never spotted Connor. Anyone else and she'd accept she might have overlooked him, but you couldn't overlook Connor Anderson. It wasn't that he was the biggest or the most gorgeous man in the room, although there was no denying he was fantasy-worthy. He simply had a presence about him. He always had. And the years hadn't done anything to diminish it.

"No. I had an appointment at the medical building down the street. Needed to have some stitches removed." He gestured toward the white bandage his short-sleeved shirt didn't completely cover.

Becca took a long sip of her iced latte. She really should eat her snack and get her butt out the door. What she should do and what she wanted to do were two very different things, however. She hadn't thought about Connor in years, but for a long time after his father's arrest and trial, she'd wondered what happened to him. Everyone who was anyone in Greenwich knew he'd gone to Harvard as planned that fall. They also knew he'd dropped out after freshman year and joined the Marines. But that was where any information pertaining to Connor ended. His parents, younger sister, and two stepsiblings were another story.

"I was over there myself. Yearly physical and blood work this morning." If he visited a doctor in the same building as hers, he either lived or worked close by. "What happened?" She pointed toward the bandage.

"Minor accident at work." He reached for his black coffee. She didn't know how anyone could drink the stuff black. She'd tried more than once but just couldn't do it. She even preferred her tea with a splash of milk and sugar, although if left with no other option she would drink it without the sugar.

"If it required stitches, it must have more than a minor accident."

In almost thirty-four years, she'd only needed stitches once. She'd been ice-skating on the lake and tripped. She'd fallen before while skating—who hadn't—but this time she whacked her chin on a chunk of ice and earned herself several stitches. She still had the faint scar to show for it.

"Trust me, I've had worse," he said before he took a sip of coffee.

His clothes gave her no hints as to the type of profession he had ended up in, so if she wanted to know, she'd have to ask. "Where do you work? Somewhere on the Hill?"

Many of the people who frequented the café worked in Washington, and those who didn't were often tourists visiting the country's capital.

"I wouldn't make it a day there. Too much—" Connor paused, but she already knew what he was thinking. And he wasn't wrong either. "—stuff I don't agree with. I'd get myself fired within hours. I'm working for Elite Force Security."

She'd heard of the fortysomething-year-old firm located in Virginia. It was considered the best private security firm in the country. Everyone from Hollywood movie stars and world-famous musicians to millionaires hired Elite Force whenever they needed bodyguards. She could easily picture people she knew, including Connor's mother and her own parents, hiring the firm—but not working for it.

I wouldn't complain about having you as a bodyguard. "I've heard they're the best out there," she said, instead of what she was really thinking.

Connor reached for the breakfast sandwich in front of him. "What about you? Do you work in D.C.?"

She watched his hands, noting the handful of scars covering them. Each one was a clear reminder he'd led a very different life since graduating high school than most of their classmates. "Yes. I took a position with Senator Lynch when he was elected four years ago."

CONNOR CLOSED his eyes momentarily and took another bite of his breakfast sandwich. There had to be at least five cafés within walking distance of the medical building, yet she'd entered the same one as him.

He'd recognized her voice the moment she asked him to pass a napkin. Becca André had been the hottest girl in high school. Hell, she'd been the hottest girl in town. And although he'd dated his fair share of girls, he'd panted after her their entire senior year. Unfortunately, for most of it, she'd been dating the class asshole, Max Shelton. When Shelton dumped her a couple days before graduation, he'd made his move. They'd never been an actual couple in his mind. However, they'd spent plenty of time together, and he'd taken things as far as she'd let him.

He hadn't seen her, though, since the night his life got turned on its friggin' head. It was a night he never thought about anymore. With Becca sitting next to him, the memories of it played across his mind like a bad B-grade movie.

He'd easily convinced her no one would care if they snuck into the pool house. Kids did it every time Leslie, Becca's best friend, threw a party at her family's house. Once inside, things moved along just as he'd hoped. He'd been about to grab the condom from his wallet when her older sister knocked, opened the door, and announced the FBI was at his house.

He'd rushed home, leaving Becca still half-dressed in the pool house. Then he kept a low profile until he moved into college. Over the next several months, he made few trips back to Connecticut.

Even before he moved into his dorm, he'd known Harvard wasn't the place for him. He'd only applied because both his father and grandfather had attended. He'd sucked it up, though, and given it a try for his grandfather's sake. By April he'd had enough of the people and politics filling the campus. He enlisted in the Marine Corps and headed to Parris Island not long after. He'd never regretted his decision either.

"Yeah, I heard he'd been elected," he said.

Connor's trips back to his home state or even New England, in general, were infrequent. His younger sister seemed to think he cared about what went on up there, though, and regularly filled him in. When the former Connecticut governor won his first term in Washington, she'd made sure to let him know.

"Do you like working for him?" He'd rather have his hand sawed off with a butter knife than work directly for one of the senators or representatives serving in Washington. But some people loved politics and wouldn't want to be anywhere else. In fact, his sister, Stephanie, was planning to get her feet wet in local politics during the next election.

"Most days," Becca admitted.

She wiped her hands on a napkin, and he noted the absence of any rings on her left hand. Actually, she didn't have on much jewelry. A decent-sized emerald on her right hand reflected the sunlight coming through the café windows, and gold hoops dangled from her ears. That was it except for her wristwatch.

"Every job has its up and downs," she continued, glancing down at her watch. "Yikes. I didn't realize it was so late." She stuffed the untouched half of her muffin back into the paper bag and added a few napkins. "I'd love to catch up more. Any chance you're free this weekend? Saturday and Sunday are both wide open for me."

If anyone else from his past sat next to him, he'd immediately say he had plans. He had no desire to catch up with anyone he'd gone to high school with. The fact that Becca André was asking had him reconsidering. He'd thought about her often during his first semester at college. More than once he'd dreamed about meeting up with her and finishing what they started the night in the pool house. A few times he'd even considered contacting her. Even after he'd learned, via his younger sister of course, that she'd started dating the son of a Canadian politician, Connor had considered it. But around the same time he decided to leave college, he'd pushed her from his thoughts. Becca, much like Harvard, belonged to a world he wanted nothing to do with.

Or at least he'd tried to push her from his thoughts. It didn't happen much anymore, but every once in a while she popped into his dreams, even now.

"Yeah, I'm free Saturday."

Her lips curved into a radiant smile, and the memory of kissing her all those summers ago snuck its way into his thoughts. *Damn, she has a beautiful smile.*

Becca pulled a business card from her purse and wrote on the back. "Both my cell and office phone numbers are on here, and I put my address on the back." She handed him the card. "We can meet somewhere, or you can pick me up." She shrugged slightly. "Actually, I could come pick you up if you want. Whatever you prefer, I'm flexible."

Connor dropped the business card into his shirt pocket. "No need. I'll come to you. One o'clock good?"

"Perfect." She gave him another smile and gathered up her things. "See you then."

He watched her exit the café and walk down the sidewalk. Outside, several men near the entrance followed her with their eyes as she passed the window. Some people didn't age well. His stepsister was a perfect example. Of course, it didn't help that Jill was constantly going under the knife and getting injections of God knew what in a futile attempt to look younger. Time had had the opposite effect on Becca. She'd been a knockout in high school. The girl all the guys wanted. The years since then hadn't changed that. Instead, they'd somehow made her hotter.

Connor took another bite of his breakfast sandwich then reached for the business card in his pocket. Flipping it over, he read the address and the note she'd added. *Looking forward to seeing you Saturday and catching up more.*

Me too, he thought. It might have been years since he'd let himself think about her, but from now until Saturday, she'd be a constant in his head.

TWO

THE BASEMENT of the firm's building housed a state-of-the-art fitness center complete with weights, cardio equipment, and a lap pool. Although it wasn't mandatory, everyone who worked for Elite Force visited the space multiple times a week rather than belong to private facilities. Regardless of the day, Connor usually went first thing in the morning. He wasn't the only one. When he walked in Saturday, several people were already using the gym.

"I thought I'd see you this morning," Keith said. He was in the process of adding additional weight plates to the forty-five-pound bar positioned over a bench. "How's it going?"

"Still living the dream," Connor answered. "What about you?"

"Can't complain now that I'm home."

"I heard you found the missing girl. Nice job."

For the past two weeks, Keith had been searching for a sixteen-year-old who had disappeared with a man she'd met on some social media site. According to the news stories Connor read, the man had originally pretended to be a high school student himself. At least that was what the missing girl's friends reported to police. It hadn't taken authorities long to discover the so-called boyfriend wasn't a teenager but in fact a twenty-eight-year-old man with a mile-long arrest record. When the parents learned the truth, they used all the resources they had to hire Elite Force Security. The assignment had immediately been turned over to HRT, and Ax assigned Keith to be the team leader.

"Yeah. Getting her out was tricky, but she's back home with her family." Keith positioned himself on the bench below the bar. "Do you mind spotting me?"

He'd asked Keith to do the same for him on numerous occasions when he bench-pressed. Somehow Connor always managed to get in one or two more reps if a buddy spotted him. The person didn't have to do a single thing but stand there with his hands just below the bar, but it always helped.

"You got it." Connor positioned himself at the head of the bench as Keith gripped the bar.

Keith punched out his first set and grabbed the water bottle on the floor. Then he moved off the bench so Connor could get in a set of reps.

"I've got an extra ticket to the ball game today. It starts at five. Baltimore is playing New York. It should be a good game," Keith said as Connor pressed the bar up one last time and racked it. "Interested in coming?"

"Get dumped again?" Connor grabbed his bottle of water and took a swig.

With a sarcastic laugh, Keith switched places with him on the bench. "You're thinking of your track record with women, not mine." Although in position, he didn't reach for the bar. "I called it quits. Sharon was getting too clingy. She wanted to move in with me. We had some fun together, but I'm not ready for a live-in girlfriend." Reaching up, he gripped the bar. "Do you want the ticket or not?"

He wasn't a Baltimore fan, but he never turned down an invitation to a baseball game. If Keith had asked him sooner, he would've accepted the ticket without any hesitation and enjoyed a night out with a buddy. As Keith lowered the bar toward his chest and back up, Connor considered the offer. He was picking Becca up at one. It was possible they'd spend less than thirty minutes together, and he'd have the rest of the day free. He had no way of knowing.

"I've got plans already. Wish you'd asked me sooner."

Keith shot him a knowing grin. "Who is she? Anyone I know?"

"Your sister." Connor waited for his friend's reaction.

"I'd have to kill you if you ever went near Jen. Not that she'd ever look twice at you. She's got good taste in men," Keith said. "Seriously, what beauty is keeping you company today? And where did you meet this one? Another waitress from Shooter's, or is it Candy again?"

Beauty describes Becca André to a T.

"I haven't seen Candy in months. I'm getting together with someone I went to high school with." Too many years had passed for him to call Becca a friend. "But if you want Candy's number, stop by the pub. I'm sure she'd give it to you." Several times over the past few months, Keith had mentioned the cute waitress from Shooter's. Connor wondered if the guy was interested in her himself.

"I don't need your leftovers."

Ready to get in his second set, Connor didn't comment as he took his place on the bench.

"Don't leave me hanging. Details. You never mention any friends from high school. This one must be either smokin' hot or special to you."

"I never said the classmate was a she," Connor said as he gripped the bar.

His friend crossed his arms over his chest and stared down at him. "If you're passing up a night of baseball, it must be a *female* classmate. So, which is it? Hot or special?"

He would only get Keith to shut up one of two ways: either punch the guy or answer him. A punch to the face while they boxed was one thing. Punching him for simply giving him a hard time was another. "Hot as hell."

Connor pictured her sitting next to him in the café. *And a little special too.*

He kept the thought safely stored in his brain. Keith would torment him for the next week if he let the little tidbit leak. And, although he'd never admit it to anyone, it was true.

Their brief involvement the summer after graduation hadn't been purely physical. He'd enjoyed the time they spent together, doing nothing but talking on the beach or mountain biking. She'd been the first girl he'd wanted to be with because he enjoyed her company rather than because he wanted to score. There hadn't been another he could honestly say he'd felt that way about since her, either.

"I'd probably pass on the ball game tonight, too, if I were you." Keith reached for his water again. "Maybe I'll see if Salty wants the ticket."

"He left for Georgia on Thursday. His family is celebrating his grandmother's one-hundredth birthday," Connor answered. "Call Mad Dog. She's a huge New York fan."

"How's she doing?"

The same attack in Paris that had left him with stitches had left Maddie with a broken leg and a few bruised ribs.

"Last time I talked to her, she was about as pleasant as a rabid dog." Connor understood his friend's crankiness. Sitting around and doing nothing didn't work for people like them. "Being stuck at home is driving her nuts. Coleman won't let her even set foot in the office until next week. And even then she'll be stuck doing support work from behind a desk until the doctor clears her."

"I'll give her a call." Keith added more weight plates to the bar. "Hot classmate, huh? How'd that happen? Got the impression you didn't bother with anyone you went to high school with. Not that I blame you. There aren't many from high school I keep in contact with, either." He slipped another plate onto the opposite side of the bar. "Where did you go to school, anyway?"

Unlike other members of the team who shared details about everything, even their childhoods, Connor never shared anything about his life before joining the Marines.

"I grew up and went to school in Connecticut." No need to share that he'd lived the first eighteen years of his life in one of the wealthiest towns in the United States. "After I got my stitches out, I went to the café down the street and bumped into Becca. She works in D.C. for some senator."

Keith positioned himself under the bar. "I'm sure you'll have more fun tonight than me." He wrapped his hands around the bar. "Ready for one last set?"

He didn't expect to have the type of fun Keith was alluding to. No way would he admit it, though. "Trust me. I plan to."

BECCA PICKED UP HER PACE. Multiple times this week she'd gotten the feeling someone was watching her. As she crossed the parking garage, it returned, making her quite glad Danny had left when she did and now walked next to her.

"Minor crisis averted," Danny said.

She nodded. When Becca had gotten the call to come in this morning, she'd feared the problem would take all day to resolve. Normally getting called in on a Saturday morning didn't bother her. After all, she'd known what she was getting into when she took the position with Senator Lynch. This morning she'd cursed all the way through her shower and into the office. She'd given Connor her number and address, but she hadn't thought to ask for his. She had no way of contacting him to reschedule their plans, and she hated the idea of standing him up if she ended up stuck at the office all day. Especially since, if she did, it would most likely mean she'd never see or hear from him again.

Thankfully, they'd come up with a solution and she should manage to at least get home before Connor arrived.

"For now anyway," she said. "It's going to need a more long-term solution at some point." She looked around the garage. All the cars appeared to be empty, and they were the only ones walking inside. Still, she couldn't shake the feeling that someone watched her.

Danny stopped between their cars. "Agreed, but now we have a little more time to come up with one." He leaned against his vehicle as she opened her car door. "I'm meeting Glynnis over at Wired for lunch. Interested in joining us?"

She regularly went out with Danny and his wife. She'd visited their home on countless occasions too. In fact, she considered them her closest friends in the area. "Thanks, but not today. I have plans this afternoon."

Calling it a date was inappropriate, even though she was more excited about this outing than she had been about any of the recent dates she'd gone on. "Sometime soon you both need to come over for dinner. It's my turn to host."

"Looking forward to it. Don't tell my wife, but you make the best chicken masala I've ever tasted. Glynnis tries, but hers doesn't even come close."

"My lips are sealed. See you Monday." Getting behind the wheel, she waved goodbye and backed out of her parking space.

As she drove toward home, the unease from inside the garage disappeared and excitement replaced it. If she'd been smart, she would've given some thought to where they should go. While they could stay at her house, she wasn't sure when Kassidy would be home. She hadn't seen her stepsister in over a week. She'd stopped home for clothes one night after work so she could spend the night at her newest boy toy's place. Before leaving, she'd mentioned she was flying out to the Lafayette laboratory in Seattle again in a few days and wasn't sure when she'd be back. Since Becca wasn't Kassidy's significant other, she hadn't pressed for answers.

It would be awful timing if Kassidy walked in the front door while Connor was visiting. She'd rather not have Kassidy ask any questions that would trigger unpleasant memories for him. She assumed he'd avoided town all these years because he wanted to bury any and all thoughts of his father's arrest and trial, and all the publicity that had accompanied both. Not that she blamed him.

When federal investigators uncovered Patrick Anderson's Ponzi scheme, they arrested him for investment fraud as well as several other federal felonies. Connor's mother might be back in the fold now, but initially, the town and many in their social circle had blackballed the entire Anderson family. Subjected to the same treatment, Becca would've left town too and never returned.

Becca watched the dark blue SUV stop outside her town house as she turned down the street. Before she reached her driveway, Connor climbed out, looking far sexier than any man should. *So much for beating him here.*

Connor was halfway up the walkway when she pulled into the driveway. When he saw her car, he stopped. Dressed in cargo shorts and a black polo shirt, and wearing sunglasses, he put every one of her recent dates to shame.

"Sorry I'm not ready," Becca said, approaching him. "Last-minute emergency at work." She paused next to him and wondered if he'd consider a hug too forward. "When Ted called me in this morning, I feared I'd be stuck at the office all day."

He removed his sunglasses and hung them near the buttons on his shirt. "You could've called and rescheduled. I would've understood."

Although every female hormone in her body screamed *touch him*, she kept her arms safely locked against her sides. "If I had your number, I probably would have. There's nothing worse than being stood up." She started toward the front door. "But I forgot to ask you for it before I left the café." *Not something I plan on forgetting today.* Unless this afternoon turned into a total disaster, she hoped to see him again.

Unlocking the door, she turned the handle. "It won't take me long to change."

She pushed the door open but hesitated when she heard an engine start. Turning, Becca watched the compact car across the street pull away from the curb. The same car had been parked there last night when she came home. It had also been there two days ago—or at least one that looked just like it had been. She hadn't taken the time to check the license plates. Now she wished she had.

As she watched the vehicle leave, she again wondered who it was. The car certainly didn't belong to the Smiths, her neighbors across the street. They didn't drive anything with a price tag under seventy-five thousand. She'd met some of the Smiths' family members and friends. None of them would be caught dead driving around in the American-made compact that had just left. Actually, she couldn't imagine any of her neighbors or their friends owning such a car. Yet this was at least the third day this week it had been in the neighborhood. The same apprehension she'd experienced in the parking garage returned.

"Is something wrong?" Connor's voice cascaded over her body, and her stomach did a backflip.

With a slight shake of her head, she stepped inside. "Just had an idea for a problem at work."

She didn't make a habit of lying, but in this case, it was preferable to admitting that the sight of a vehicle made her uneasy. Especially to a guy like Connor. He'd served in the military and now worked as a personal bodyguard. Someone like that would never let the sight of a car make them uneasy.

After Connor entered, she closed and locked the door. "Make yourself comfortable. If you want a drink, the kitchen is down the hall on the left. I'll be right back."

Upstairs, she didn't even bother to add her skirt to the bag intended for the dry cleaners. Instead, she left both her skirt and blouse on the bed, pulled on some shorts and a T-shirt, then grabbed a pair of sandals from the closet. She paused just long enough to check her reflection in the mirror before leaving the room. If she had more time, she'd touch up her makeup, but with company downstairs she simply moved on.

Connor stood near a window in the living room when she got back downstairs.

"Anything interesting going on out there?" she asked.

He turned toward her, his eyes giving her the once-over. "Quiet as a cemetery. Not even a car has gone by."

"Trust me, it's not usually like that, but I never complain when it is. After spending each and every day in D.C., I need some peace and quiet."

She considered her favorite armchair, the one she usually went for when she wanted to relax with a good book and a cup of tea. If she sat there today, she'd be alone. The chair was certainly wide enough for two, but Connor would never join her there. On the other hand, if she took a seat on the sofa, Connor might sit next to her rather than in one of the other seats. If he were next to her, it'd be easy enough to accidentally brush against him, something she wasn't above doing if it meant she could touch him.

Yep, the sofa was the place to sit today.

As she'd hoped, he sat next to her. "Do you live here alone?" he asked.

Tucking one leg under her, Becca turned so she faced him. "Until this past spring I did. My stepsister technically lives with me, although she's away a lot more than she's here."

Connor's gaze searched the room before settling on her again. "Which one?"

Was he asking because he really needed to ask, or to be polite? It didn't seem like he'd ask to be polite, but how could he not know her stepsister Sylvia had married Benjamin Rowe, the son of media mogul Bruce Rowe. It'd been all over the internet and in every tabloid magazine at the time.

"Kassidy. Sylvia is married and has two little girls," Becca answered. "What about you? Do you live alone?"

If he was living with a girlfriend, she doubted he would've agreed to see her today. Then again, maybe he would've. She hadn't said the word date when she asked to see him today, and even people in relationships could see friends of the opposite sex. How many times had she and Danny gone for a drink after work? And he was married.

"Yeah. A buddy from work stayed with me for a few months while his new place was being built. Spike moved out back in March."

"I hope Spike is a nickname."

He gave her smile that had her stomach doing some back-flips again. "It is. His real name is Jonathan. I don't know how he got the name Spike, but it's what everyone calls him."

"That's a relief. People give their children some crazy names."

"Trust me, I've heard worse than Spike."

Connor's cell phone ringing stopped her from speaking. She watched the muscles in his arm move as he reached into his shorts pocket. Rock-hard and well-defined described them. He obviously spent a decent amount of time working out. How would it feel to have them around her? How would it feel to have him holding her tightly against his body like he had the night in the pool house? She didn't need to see him naked to know he'd physically outshine her most recent boyfriend. Even their senior year of high school, the other guys had looked like preadolescent boys compared to him. So much so, she could still remember the first time she'd seen him without a shirt. It'd actually been the summer before their senior year. He'd showed up at the last-minute pool party her best friend, Leslie, had decided to throw while her parents were away. She'd been sitting outside with her boyfriend, Max, when Connor and a few other football players pulled off their shirts and jumped into the pool. Although Max had been next to her, Becca hadn't been able to keep her eyes off Connor. And she hadn't been the only girl present unable to look away. If he pulled off his shirt now, she'd find herself in the same situation.

"Sorry about that. Junk call."

His voice shook her from her pleasant trip down memory lane. When she was alone later, she'd have to revisit and perhaps imagine how his body had improved since then. "I get them all the time too. It drives me nuts." She pushed the annoying strand of hair that had escaped her ponytail back behind her ear. "I haven't eaten all day. Are you hungry?"

"Getting there. I grabbed a protein shake before I left my house."

"There's a fabulous sandwich shop a few streets over. We could get something to go and bring it over to the park."

She loved eating outside regardless of the weather. Even on chilly fall days, she often brought her breakfast or dinner out to the deck on the roof. She'd suggest they make something here and go up there instead of the park, but she had nothing but fruit, a head of lettuce, and some mustard in the fridge. Not even a gourmet chef would be able to make anything tasty out of those ingredients.

"Sounds like a plan. Lead the way."

***

HE'D NEVER BEEN MORE grateful for sunglasses than he was now. The dark shades let him watch Becca with her none the wiser. At the moment, his eyes feasted on her delectable ass as she bent to spread out the blanket she'd brought along for their picnic. When she finished, she turned, depriving him of the view he'd been enjoying, and took one of the multiple bags he held.

"I'm surprised it's not busier here today." Becca sat on the blanket. "On the weekends, this place is usually full of people. Maybe it's too hot."

He sure as hell was hot, but it wasn't all due to the weather.

His internal temperature had jumped ten degrees the moment he saw her walk toward him outside her town house. Even being inside the home with its central air conditioning hadn't helped.

"You come here a lot?" If he kept them both talking, he might get through lunch without kissing her. But that was a big if.

When he accepted her invitation, he'd expected it to be a one-and-done kind of day. He'd see her, do a little catching up, and then they'd go their separate ways for another fifteen or twenty years. His thoughts had been deviating from the plan since he walked into her house. Exactly how far they'd deviate was still in the air, but tasting her lips at least once seemed like an excellent addition to the plan.

"Whenever I can. I like to run here. I find it more relaxing than running on the sidewalk or on the gym's treadmill."

His eyes traveled up from her lilac-painted toenails to the hem of her shorts, and an image of them in bed with her legs wrapped around him formed. "You were on the cross-country team in high school." He didn't know how but he remembered she'd run cross-country in the fall and played tennis in the spring.

Becca nodded, the same piece of mahogany-colored hair she'd been pushing behind her ear since she came downstairs falling free again. Before she could move it, he did.

"I was on the cross-country team at Georgetown too." She handed him his sandwich before pulling out her own. "Working for the senator takes up most of my time during the week, but I like to come here and run on the weekends. At least until it gets too cold. Then I settle for the treadmill at the gym."

She leaned forward, and her neckline dipped just enough to provide him with an excellent view of her cleavage. The mere sight had his blood going from simple simmer to full boil. When she sat up and readjusted her top, he mentally reached out, tugged it down again, and then closed his hands around her breasts. Since what his mind was telling him to do was out of the question, at least for the moment, he unwrapped his sandwich instead. A definite poor substitute for what his hands really wanted.

"What about you?" Becca asked. "Do you still do a lot of hiking? You used to go skiing a lot too."

Except during football season, he'd spent many weekends hiking as a teenager. Sometimes he'd go with friends and other times he'd go alone. It'd been almost a year since he'd last gone. It'd been even longer since he'd strapped on a pair of skis.

"I hike when I can," Connor answered. "Last time I skied I was at Harvard." He'd skied more because his family enjoyed it and regularly took vacations to the best ski resorts in the country than because he'd loved the sport.

"I haven't skied in ages myself. I loved it when I was younger, but for some reason, the last few times I went, I didn't enjoy myself." She licked a dab of mayo off her finger, and he wished she was using her tongue on him instead. "My last boyfriend enjoyed hiking, so we used to go a lot."

Last boyfriend. He interpreted her statement to mean she wasn't involved with anyone. He wasn't looking for a woman in his life, but he wouldn't refuse a few fun months with Becca either.

"Things between Tate and me ended not long after I moved down here to work for the senator. The distance made having any kind of relationship too difficult. So I guess it's been about four years since I last hiked." She grabbed a potato chip from the bag sitting between them. "I wouldn't mind doing it again."

She popped the chip into her mouth and chewed before speaking again. "Actually, the first time I ever went hiking was with you. We went to Bear Mountain State Park in New York. Do you remember? It was so darn hot that day."

Connor remembered. They'd hiked until they found an isolated spot with a superb view of the Hudson River. Then they'd stayed there, talking when they weren't making out. He hadn't been back to the park since.

"There are some decent hiking places not far from here," Connor said. "If you're interested, I'll show you."

"Sounds...." Becca paused and rubbed her arm, her eyes sweeping the area.

"Something wrong?" He dropped his sandwich on the paper it had come wrapped in.

"No, I don't think so. But I suddenly got this feeling like someone's watching me."

Connor surveyed the area. Several yards away a family of four sat, enjoying a picnic. Across from them, a group of guys tossed around a Frisbee while at the same time subjecting Becca to a thorough visual inspection. Further away a bunch of kids played soccer while their parents cheered them on. Several joggers went by and looked Becca's way as they passed. Then there was the punk on a bench, wearing a sleeveless T-shirt with a rock band's name on the front, talking on his cell phone. Although the dude was definitely checking Becca out, he wasn't raising any red flags in Connor's head.

She cleared her throat and shrugged. "I'm probably just being paranoid."

"No, you're not. Half the guys in the park are looking at you and wishing they sat where I am." *And they're fantasizing that you're naked and in bed with them.* "If I was in their shoes, I'd be looking at you too." *And having very similar fantasies.*

Becca gave him a slight nudge in the arm and smiled. "I'm going to take that as a compliment. And to answer you, yes, I'm interested in doing some hiking."

He picked his sandwich up again and watched a blonde chick sit on the punk's lap. She might be a good ten years younger than Becca, but she couldn't compete with her in the looks department. Of course, not many women could. "Before I leave, we can decide on a day and time."

THREE

Dale Fuller pulled his tie off and tossed it over a chair. He'd spent the majority of the day listening to old men bitch and whine. Unfortunately, the same old men were among the biggest contributors to his first campaign—and he needed them, or at least their money and influence, for his upcoming one. After turning the air conditioner down a few more degrees, he entered his bedroom and went straight to the framed picture hanging near the bed. If anyone else entered the room, they might admire it for a moment or two, but then they'd turn their attention to the fabulous view of the city the windows provided—exactly as he'd intended when he'd bought the condo and then had it redecorated.

He pushed the black-and-white picture aside, revealing the wall safe hidden behind it, and punched in the code. After removing the three burner phones from inside, he closed the safe and slid the picture back into place.

Dale first switched on the phone he'd been using to communicate with Rick, the private investigator he'd hired. Rick had been searching for a little over a week and still hadn't turned up anything. He didn't expect to get a different answer this afternoon either, but he'd call and check. When Rick again delivered nothing, Dale would fire him and fall back on plan B.

"Any updates?" he asked when Rick answered the phone.

"Afraid not, Congressman Fuller. She hasn't been on social media, and we haven't been able to track her cell. We tried watching the laboratory, but security outside threatened to call the cops if we didn't leave."

He could've told Rick that would happen if they lingered too long outside Lafayette Laboratory. Security there was tight. Even the employee parking lot required a special access card to enter, never mind the main entrance to the building.

"Like we discussed, I tried following her sister this week, hoping she'd meet up with your ex. Nothing," Rick continued. "One of my associates tried watching her house, but there have been no signs of your ex there either. We did get a picture of a man who visited the sister over the weekend. If you want us to find out who he is, we can."

Becca André was Kassidy's stepsister, not her sister, but correcting Rick was a moot point. And he didn't care who Becca spent her free time with unless it was Kassidy Buchanan.

"Do you want me to keep looking?" Rick asked.

Wouldn't you love it if I said yes? The private investigator wasn't cheap, especially considering he hadn't uncovered even a hint of where Kassidy was. "No. I think it's time I accept she and my money are long gone and move on."

"I'm sorry we couldn't find her," Rick said, clear disappointment in his voice. Rick and his associates were well known for being both discreet and successful. Of course, most of the time they were following cheating spouses or snapping pictures of people trying to fake life-altering injuries for big paydays. They weren't trying to track down individuals who didn't want to be located.

"Me too." *Just not for the reasons you think.*

Dale ended the call and pulled the battery from the cheap disposable phone. After removing the SIM card, he snapped the device in half and returned everything to the safe. Later he would dispose of the individual pieces at various places, but for now, the safe would be a good place to store them.

Reaching for the second one, he pressed the power button. The last messages he'd received from Kassidy had come almost three weeks ago. At the time, she'd promised she'd be in contact again soon, but she hadn't called or messaged him since. Considering the timetable they were working with, he'd expected another message two weeks ago, which was why he'd hired Rick when Kassidy remained dark.

He didn't expect to have any messages tonight, either. But before he gave Zane the go-ahead, he'd check because he considered using the guy a last resort.

Tonight, like the last dozen times he powered on the phone, there were no texts or voice messages waiting for him. "Damn it, Kassidy. Where the hell are you?" He switched off the device and tossed it back into the safe too.

Grabbing the last burner phone, he dropped his personal cell phone on the nightstand, left his condo, and headed for a popular coffee shop several blocks away. Using a burner phone meant the authorities wouldn't be able to trace a specific phone number back to him. That was why he always used disposable devices for contacting the private investigator and Kassidy. While he'd rather there not be any record of his calls to Rick or Kassidy, he knew the police wouldn't be looking into the calls they received and then searching for where the calls originated, so calling them from his condo was safe. There was no guarantee where Zane was concerned.

If the police went after Zane again for any one of his criminal activities, they'd search everything from the thug's bank accounts to his phone records. From there it would be easy for them to determine what numbers had called Zane and then approximate where the phone had been at the time of the call or text message. Dale didn't want them tracing the location back to his condo. In the past, he could've said it was a simple conversation between attorney and client. He had been the lead defense attorney during Zane's last trial. However, as a congressman, he was no longer practicing law, so the excuse wouldn't hold up and the police would dig further. If that happened, there was plenty they might uncover, ending not only his time in Congress but also his life as a free man.

With a large coffee in hand, Dale sat and called his former client.

Zane answered on the third ring.

"It's Fuller."

"Expected to hear from you sooner," Zane said in his all-too-familiar gravelly voice, the one that said the guy smoked at least two packs a day and had been for a long time.

"Start with the house. I want every computer device in it. You know where to deliver the stuff." Dale sipped his coffee and watched an attractive redhead wearing a super short skirt and a halter top walk past his table toward the counter. "If I don't find what I need on them, we'll proceed as we discussed. You'll have free rein to do whatever you need. But remember, only if I don't get the information I need."

"Anything?" Zane asked.

When people reached a certain point of desperation, they did what they had to. He'd reached his. "Anything. I want both. However, if I can only have one, bring me the information and do what you want with the other."

In the long run, the information would bring him the money he wanted, but the woman wouldn't. And at this point, he didn't care what happened to Kassidy Buchanan or anyone associated with her.

FOUR

"LONG DAY?" Keith asked Monday night.

"Hell, yeah," Connor replied. He'd spent several hours seated in a run-down apartment listening to Neil Foley's wire in case he needed backup. In an effort to bring down a violent Baltimore-based organization that'd been pimping out girls as young as fourteen while also making sure the drug problem in the city continued, Neil had gone undercover.

Originally, the parents of a girl who'd been lured away from home by the organization had contacted Elite Force. The firm had quickly partnered with the local authorities, though, to not only get all the girls safely back to their parents but to also eradicate the organization once and for all.

Neil had immediately volunteered for the assignment. He'd been working for months to get in close to the leaders. Today had been Neil's first face-to-face with the organization's second-in-command. Although Connor would take a bullet if it meant helping anyone who worked for the firm, he'd prefer to be the one infiltrating the organization while someone else sat around and listened to the meetings.

"Could be worse. You could be stuck escorting Stan Bonds," Keith said. "He hired us for another of his trips to Venezuela."

A bigmouth oil guy from Texas, Stan frequently hired Elite Force to keep his sorry ass safe when he traveled outside the country. Connor had never dealt with the dude, but he knew guys who had, and none of them had anything nice to say about him. "Again? He can't be going down there only for business."

Keith laughed. "Depends on what kind of business you're talking about."

Connor locked up the equipment he'd used today. Keeping a mistress in a different country might make it harder for the guy's wife to find out, but it must be costing Bonds a fortune considering the number of times he'd hired the firm to accompany him down there.

"Did your plans on Saturday carry over into Sunday?"

He hadn't seen Keith since Saturday morning in the gym. "No."

"Strike out? Happens to everyone. Not me, of course, but don't worry about it." Keith pushed open the door to the stairwell. "How about we hit the bar? Grab a few beers and maybe find some new friends for the night."

"Not tonight."

"Feeling okay?" Keith asked, sounding surprised.

In the past, he'd join Keith for a beer and more than likely bring a woman back to his place for a few hours. After spending the day with Becca, the idea of having any other woman but her in his bed held no appeal whatsoever—a fact he should be concerned about, because his normal stance when it came to women was that one was just as good as the next.

"Got something else in mind." He didn't know whether she had plans for the night or not, but Becca had occupied his thoughts since he left her house. Waiting until the weekend to see her again wasn't an option. Another thing he should examine further but wouldn't.

"Then you didn't strike out with the hot classmate you saw over the weekend."

Talking about their sexual exploits wasn't unusual. Tonight

he had no desire to share what had or hadn't happened between him and Becca. "See you later, Wallace."

"Don't do anything I wouldn't," Keith called out as Connor walked away.

Connor pressed her contact info as he slid behind the steering wheel. There was no point in driving to her house and dealing with the traffic if she wasn't home. It rang several times before she answered.

"Any plans for tonight?" he asked after she greeted him.

"Uh, no."

"Good. Do you want some company?"

"I'm not home yet. But I'll be leaving work in a few minutes."

Eight o'clock and still at the office. He didn't know about the politicians who parked their asses on the Hill, but evidently, their workers put in long days. "Leaving work now too. By the time you get home, I'll be there. I can grab us dinner on the way."

He heard the rustling of papers in the background before Becca answered. "That would be great."

"Do you like barbeque?" When it came to food, he wasn't overly picky, but tonight he felt like ribs.

"Yes."

"I'll stop at Cooper's Smokehouse and pick up some food." He'd learned of the place when he worked as Allison Sher-brooke's bodyguard. It wasn't far from Becca's house in Alexandria and had awesome food.

WHEN BECCA OPENED THE DOOR, she was balancing a cell phone between her shoulder and ear while holding a compact-sized laptop. She gestured for him to come in then walked away and into a room down the hall, leaving him alone in the foyer.

He remembered her saying the kitchen was down the hall, so he headed in that direction. The room he entered was two or three times the size of his kitchen and reminded him of the one at his younger sister's house, right down to the large floral arrangement on the table.

The restaurant had added paper plates and plastic utensils to the takeout bag. Rather than search through the cabinets, Connor pulled those out and set the table while he waited. If Becca had a problem using them—hell, he knew his mother wouldn't be caught dead using a plastic fork—she could get what she wanted when she joined him.

He only managed to get the Memphis ribs out before she walked in the room, her heels clicking against the tiles announcing her arrival.

"Whatever you picked out for dinner smells great. Thanks for grabbing something."

He watched her cross the room, still dressed in the outfit she'd worn to work. The dress hugged her curves like a glove and ended a couple of inches below the knee, depriving him of the full view of her legs.

She paused at the fridge. "I was going to open wine when I got home, but I think beer goes better with barbeque. Can I get you one? I'll save the wine for after dinner."

Becca André kept beer in the house. He never would've guessed it. "Please."

"So, what did you get us tonight?" she asked.

As she approached, a bottle of beer in each hand, he considered the downside to pushing her up against the kitchen island, slipping his hands under her clothes, and kissing her while he undressed her.

"Regardless of what else you got, I hope there's some corn bread." She handed him a bottle, the glass incredibly cold compared to the fire burning inside him.

He took a swig from the bottle before he did anything that might have Becca tossing him out on his ass, depriving him of both her company and his dinner. "A meal from Cooper's wouldn't be complete without corn bread." He pulled the order of corn bread out and set it on the table. "We also have Memphis ribs, pulled pork, sliced brisket, and pulled chicken. I got a bunch of sides too."

Becca gathered up the plates he'd set out. "Unless you want to stay in here, I'd like to eat out on the deck." She put the plates back into the bag closest to her.

He had a plastic container in his hand, but he let it go. "Doesn't matter to me where we eat."

What she called a deck he considered a living room, minus the walls and a ceiling. Located on top of the home's lowest roof, the space was nicer than some of the rooms in his house. Various pieces of furniture had been perfectly positioned throughout the area. A bar that contained a sink with running water occupied the space closest to the door leading onto the deck. A fireplace filled the far-left corner, and several chairs, as well as a love seat, were placed around it. Numerous potted plants, most of which he couldn't identify, were stationed around the rooftop getaway, completing the luxurious atmosphere and helping a person forget they remained in the city.

"The view would've been better if the builders put the deck up there." Becca pointed to the roof covering the highest part of the three-story home. "But I think they picked this spot because it's a little more private, and it's directly over the kitchen." After leaving the things she'd carried out on the glass table, she went to switch on the gas fireplace.

When she turned and walked back toward him, Connor couldn't tear his eyes from the movement of her hips. "I think the view is perfect."

She stopped about a foot from him, and her eyes scanned his face. Then one corner of her mouth inched upward. "Yeah, it is rather nice."

IT'D BEEN one of those days where nothing seemed to go right. When she'd finally gotten the opportunity to leave, all she could think about was some time alone. Even before she turned off her computer, she'd mapped out her itinerary for the night. The moment she got home, she'd slip into the hot tub for some much-needed peace and quiet. When she started to turn into a raisin, she'd get out, pour a glass of wine, and retreat out to the deck with whatever leftovers she found in the fridge. At least, those had been her plans until Connor called. As much as she'd craved a night of solitude, she'd wanted to see him even more. Their time on Saturday had gone by much quicker than she would've liked, and their upcoming hike seemed like a lifetime away.

"Do you always work so late?" Connor asked as he proceeded to pile as much food as he could onto the paper plate he'd pulled from one of the bags.

Eager to see if the food tasted as good as it smelled, she added a little of everything to her plate, including the collard greens which, depending on what restaurant made them, could be delicious or downright disgusting. "Not every night, but it's not unusual either."

She lifted a rib to her mouth and tore off a chunk of meat. Unless she was eating either a sandwich or pizza, she preferred to use a fork when she ate. Unfortunately, she saw no practical way to do that with the ribs. And although she didn't usually eat them for that exact reason, they looked too good to pass up tonight.

The sweet and tangy meat all but melted in her mouth. "Wow," she said, raising the rib toward her mouth again. "Where did you get these again? They're amazing." He'd mentioned where he planned to get takeout, but she didn't remember the name. She pulled off another mouthful while she waited for an answer.

Across from her, Connor had already polished off a rib and started on the brisket. "Cooper's Smokehouse. It's about ten or fifteen minutes from here." He shoved a forkful of food into his mouth.

She ran through all the restaurants she could think of around her, but she couldn't remember ever seeing a place called Cooper's Smokehouse. "I don't think I've ever noticed it." Becca licked the barbecue sauce off her thumb and said a little thank-you that her mom wasn't there to tell her how unladylike it was.

"Yeah, unless you're looking for it, the place is easy to miss."

"How did you find it?" She reached for a mini loaf of corn bread. "Is it near your house?" They never discussed where he lived these days.

"About a year ago, Elite Force was hired by a member of the Sherbrooke family. They gave me the assignment, and she didn't live far from here."

He didn't have to say anymore. "You're talking about Allison Sherbrooke." She remembered the headlines. A stalker had broken into the woman's home. Although her boyfriend had suffered some injuries, only the intruder had died that night.

Connor nodded. "She loves barbecue. Got takeout from Cooper's several times while I worked for her."

Although they attended similar society events, somehow she'd never met Allison. She had met her cousin Sara, President Sherbrooke's youngest daughter, though. Actually, she'd seen Sara and her husband, Christopher Hall, at a Clean Water Matters fundraiser back in the spring.

"I remember reading about what happened to her. I can't image going through something like she did." Somehow knowing it had taken place so close to her made it even worse. She could walk to Cameron Street in less than ten minutes. "I wasn't surprised when I saw the house go on the market. After all that, I wouldn't want to live there either."

Between the police tape outside the home and the shots of it on the news after the incident, she'd known exactly which house was Allison's.

"It wouldn't bother me," Connor admitted. "But she never stayed in the house again. It took a while for the place to sell."

Regardless of how beautiful a home, a lot of buyers, herself included, would be turned off by the fact that a man had died a violent death in the master bedroom. Call her silly, but even if a person had passed away peacefully in the bedroom, she'd rather not live in the house. "You're still in contact with her?"

Just because she'd never met the woman didn't mean she didn't know what Allison looked like. The media loved to print pictures of everyone in the Sherbrooke family, Allison included. The woman was beautiful. Although completely irrational, the idea of Connor being close enough to Allison to know just how long it'd taken her to sell a house had Becca grinding her teeth.

Connor washed down his food with some beer before he answered. "I've seen her a few times since then."

Her unwarranted jealously inched closer to the surface, and she reached for her own drink.

"Her boyfriend, Rock, is a good friend of mine. We were in the Marine Corps together. I tried to get him to come work with me, but he wouldn't budge."

"They're still together?" Rock wasn't the most common of names, and she remembered it from the news articles last year.

"They've been living together since last year." He added another helping of pulled pork to his plate and went for his fork again. "Last time Rock and I talked, he was shopping for an engagement ring. Don't know if he found one or not."

The fact he only still saw Allison because she was dating one of his friends helped dismiss the jealousy she knew she shouldn't be feeling but did. "When he proposes, I'm sure it'll be in all the magazines and all over the internet."

He nodded and dug into the collard greens. "I like Allison, but I wouldn't want to be involved with anyone named Sherbrooke. The media doesn't leave the family alone. I'd go insane living like that."

BECCA TOPPED off Connor's wineglass before pouring what was left of the bottle into hers. Next to her, Connor sat with his legs stretched out and his head tilted. The outside lights remained off, but between the moon and the light from the fireplace, she could clearly see him. Since he seemed more focused on the stars, she let her eyes do as they pleased.

Earlier, when they'd been talking about the view, she assumed he hadn't meant the landscape around them. She definitely hadn't.

The man was too handsome for his own good, but like in high school, there was something besides his appearance drawing her to him. In an odd sort of way, he reminded her of the white knight depicted in fairy tales. The one who rode in, swept the damsel in distress off her feet, and carried her back to his castle so they could have their happily ever after. Considering what he did for a living, he could certainly rescue any woman in need. As far as bringing her back to his castle so they could spend their lives together, she wasn't sure.

The Connor she'd known years ago had been like a lot of teenage boys. He'd dated and, if rumors were true, slept with half the cheerleading squad. She couldn't remember him ever staying with one girl longer than a few weeks. Some people grew out of such behavior and eventually settled down. Others, like her stepsister for example, never did. While she wanted to get acquainted with Connor again, she didn't want to let her emotions get too involved like she had years ago and then have him suddenly say *adios*. She wouldn't have labeled what she felt for Connor that summer as love, but it'd been pretty darn close. If they'd spent much more time together back then, it probably would've been. If she'd fallen for him before, she knew it could happen again. How, Becca couldn't say, but she knew if she fell for him again and it ended as abruptly as before, it would hurt even more this time around.

"I'm glad you called tonight," she said.

Connor looked away from the stars and at her.

Becca briefly wondered if she should share her thoughts. *Take the plunge*, she told herself. *You only live once.* "I've thought about you a lot since Saturday."

The smile he gave her nearly melted her into a puddle of warm liquid goo. Instead of sharing whatever might be going on in his head, he leaned toward her, his intention obvious, and her mind shouted, "Show me what you've learned since high school."

"Hey, Becca," a voice said from across the deck, and Connor stopped his lips a breath away from hers.

The moment ruined, she looked toward the doorway leading back into the house. "Kassidy, you're home." She'd never regretted having a roommate more than at this very second. "When did you get back from Seattle?"

Kassidy crossed the deck toward them. "Yesterday, but I spent last night at Bryan's."

So that was the name of her stepsister's latest sexual partner. Considering how quickly Kassidy went through men, Becca really couldn't label any guy she got involved with as a boyfriend.

"Oh," Becca said, taking in Kassidy's appearance and suppressing the urge to say, "What the heck did you do to your hair?"

The last time she'd stopped home for clothes, Kassidy's dirty-blonde hair had hung well past her shoulders to almost the middle of her back. Tonight she was sporting an auburn-colored pixie cut. "You changed your hair again." Naturally a brunette, Kassidy changed her hair color regularly, although she'd never worn it quite so short. Honestly, the shorter style didn't look good on her.

"I needed a change." As if she wasn't intruding, she took a seat in one of the chairs near them. "When I came up, I didn't realize you had company."

Yeah, right. Kassidy couldn't have missed Connor's SUV. She'd known Becca had company and had come up to investigate because Kassidy was and always had been nosy. As far as Becca was concerned, it was her most annoying trait, and one Kassidy should've grown out of a long time ago.

Kassidy turned her attention in Connor's direction. "Hey, Connor. Becca mentioned she ran into you recently. How have you been?"

As Connor and Kassidy exchanged greetings, she considered the ramifications of tossing her stepsister off the deck so they could get back to more interesting activities.

FIVE

THEY PASSED the visitor center for Catoctin Mountain Park and pulled into the already-crowded parking lot. It looked like they weren't the only ones who thought hiking the mountain was a good way to spend a beautiful Saturday. She'd certainly been looking forward to this outing ever since Connor offered to take her hiking. Actually, the thought of seeing him again today had occupied her thoughts since he left her house Monday night.

"Have you hiked here before?" Becca got out of the car, grateful for a chance to stretch her legs. They hadn't hit too much traffic on the highway, but the drive from her house to the mountain in Maryland had still taken about an hour and forty-five minutes.

"A few times. Regardless of traffic, it takes me over two hours to get here from where I live, so I usually stick with places closer to me." Connor opened the trunk and pulled out a back-pack. "You can toss your water bottle or anything else you want in here. I packed a couple extras just in case. I didn't know what you liked, so I brought some high-protein bars and dried fruit too."

Becca had checked her closet and Kassidy's this morning for a backpack, or any other suitable bag for today, but had come up empty-handed. She was glad Connor had brought one along, so she didn't have to carry her bottle all day.

"I like both. And I brought some granola bars." She reached back into the SUV and grabbed the plastic grocery bag she'd left on the floor. "I thought we might be hungry after and could eat them in the car. Maybe we should toss them in the backpack too."

Connor added the bars and her water to the bag and zipped it closed. "What are you up for today? This place has everything from easy to tough trails." He put his arms through the straps.

She considered herself in good shape, but it had been a long time since she'd walked up anything but a paved sidewalk on a hilly street. "How about something in the middle?"

"Let's grab a map inside. It'll list the difficulty of each trail."

He slipped his sunglasses back on and slammed the trunk closed. The movement caused the muscles in his arms to flex, and she wondered what it might take to get him to put them around her before the day was out. She'd been having similar thoughts most of the week. A guy's arms had always been one of the first things she noticed about him. That and his eyes. Eyes told you a lot about a person. Since Connor's were again covered, she'd settle for looking at his arms—and if she found herself walking behind him, she wasn't above checking out his butt too. She'd indulged in a good long stare at the park Saturday when he'd crossed the grass to dispose of their trash. If given the opportunity again today, she'd take it. Most women she knew would as well.

Feeling his arms around her wasn't the only thing she'd fantasized about this week either. Having sex with him had occupied a decent amount of her time as well. Kassidy's sudden appearance on the rooftop had killed whatever mood was developing Monday night. She didn't know exactly why it hadn't returned after Kassidy went back inside, but it hadn't. Yeah, he'd kissed her before he left, but it hadn't even come close to satisfying what she really wanted and what she'd thought he wanted, too, before her stepsister had appeared. Afterward, she'd spent a good hour in bed cursing first Kassidy for interrupting them and then herself for not just making the first move and inviting him to spend the night—something she'd never done since moving to the D.C. area.

When they reached the visitor center's door, he opened it for her. "You never did mention where you live." Becca stepped inside. They'd shared a lot during their time together, but the exact location of his home hadn't been among the details. Since he worked for Elite Force Security, which was located just outside of D.C., she assumed he lived perhaps not in Alexandria but at least in the same general area as she did.

Connor stopped in front of the large map hanging on the wall and took a guide. "Still over in Dumfries. It was convenient when I was stationed at Quantico. It's not the best commute, but prices for anything closer to the office are ridiculous."

Connor's family had taken a major financial hit following his father's arrest and prosecution, but they hadn't been left destitute. His paternal grandfather, a graduate of Harvard Law and a Los Angeles attorney who had represented some of Hollywood's biggest names, and his wife still hosted incredibly lavish parties in both their New York and Beverly Hills homes. A man like him would've set up trust funds for his grandchildren. Trust funds the government wouldn't have been able to touch after Patrick Anderson's conviction. She didn't know as much about his maternal grandparents. However, she'd seen them at more than one fundraiser during Senator Lynch's campaign, so they traveled in the same social circles as her parents. If Connor wanted a place closer to work, it should be within his ability, unless he'd cut himself off not only from everyone in town but his family and anything associated with them as well.

"I'm not sure I've been out that way." Considering the amount of free time she had, she rarely traveled far from home without a good reason. "How far is it from me?"

Around them, more people entered the visitor center. Some

headed for the restrooms, but others crowded around the trail map. Becca noticed more than one woman cast an appreciative glance Connor's way.

"Let's look at this outside." He held up the folded trail guide.

She fully supported his idea.

Once surrounded by nothing but fresh air he said, "Depends on traffic. Today it only took me forty minutes to get to your place. During the week it'd be a minimum of an hour."

Connor unfolded the map and held it so they could both see the various lines crossing the mountain. Each line was marked by a colored blaze that corresponded to the key at the bottom. The key listed the name of the trail, its length, difficulty level, and the estimated time it would take to complete it. "Thoughts?"

Becca studied the picture and the key below. She skipped over the hikes marked as easy and jumped down to the section listing the moderate ones. It might be ridiculous, but she didn't want Connor thinking she was so out of shape she couldn't handle more than a leisurely stroll through the woods.

The Cunningham Falls Nature trail immediately jumped out at her because, according to the description, it would take them by the largest cascading waterfall in Maryland. She'd always found something about running or falling water peaceful. Unfortunately, the last sentence in the paragraph mentioned it was the most popular trail in the park. She'd prefer to not be disturbed too much while she enjoyed nature and, more importantly, Connor's company.

"How about this one?" She pointed to the description for the Thurmont Vista Loop. The guide listed it as a moderate hike that would take them to the Thurmont Vista Overlook. The overlook had an elevation of 1,499 feet and would provide them with an excellent view of the area. That was assuming she could tear her eyes away from the view of Connor Anderson. Honestly, she wasn't sure she'd be able to manage it today—or any other day for that matter.

"Looks good to me," he said, folding the map back up and sticking it in a side pocket of his backpack.

Leaving the center and crowd behind, they started on the trail. At the beginning, it was wide enough for them to walk side by side. Soon it narrowed, making that impossible, and Connor stopped. "Do you want to take the lead?" he asked.

She enjoyed being in charge, but allowing him to take the lead at least for now would give her the perfect opportunity to admire him. She couldn't do any admiring if he was walking behind her. "Why don't you do it now, and we can switch later."

With a slight nod, he started off again.

"When you need a rest or a drink, just say the word," Connor called over his shoulder. "Don't wait for me to stop."

Her mouth suddenly went dry as her eyes followed his sexy jean-clad butt, and she considered asking for her water then and there. Instead, she fished a Vitamin C drop from her front pocket and popped it into her parched mouth.

"If you weren't here with me today, what would you be doing?" Becca asked as she followed him around a fallen tree.

"Depends. I might be working. My job often includes nights and weekends." Connor's voice drifted back to her. "If I'm not on an assignment, I hang with friends or hit the gym. Occasionally I'll go to a baseball or football game."

She doubted the man lived as a monk. He hadn't mentioned it, but he must date. Again she wondered if he played the field like he had in high school, sleeping with a different woman every weekend. Or had he outgrown that and now gravitated toward stable, long-term relationships? Becca had always preferred the stable type. Yeah, she'd been out with numerous men thanks to all the blind dates her brother and other friends liked to set her up on, but she hadn't slept with any of them. The only men she'd been intimate with had been those she'd been in serious relationships with. She'd never gone straight from dinner to a guy's bed in her life, which meant she hadn't had sex in four long years. Considering their past, she would go straight from this mountain hike to Connor's, though.

"What about you?" he asked.

Becca watched the way his jeans stretched across his butt as he climbed up on a large boulder on the path and wished she had a fan handy. When he straightened, he turned and held his hand down to her.

"Sometimes I'll see friends." She accepted his help and climbed up. "My dad and stepmom visit the area a lot. When they're around, I'll see them. And my sister and Max come to D.C. about once a month or so, and we usually get together." She hoped by mentioning her family, he'd open up a little about his. She'd avoided the topic but was dying to know more about his current relationship with his parents and sister.

"Max?" Connor asked.

She nodded. "Max Shelton, Giselle's fiancé. They're getting married this November. He graduated with us."

"Oh, I remember the jerk," he said. "You dated him most of our senior year."

She tried not to think about the time she'd spent with Max. Although not quite as full of himself now as he had been back then, the man still considered himself far superior to everyone else. She didn't know how she'd managed to be with him for so long in high school, or how her older sister managed to be around him now. The only plausible explanation Becca could come up with was that Max behaved differently when he and Giselle were alone.

"Please don't remind me." She stepped in front of him and started walking again. If she stayed walking behind him much longer, she was going to self-combust and possibly burn down the entire forest. "I'll take the lead for a while."

Connor chuckled and followed her. "I couldn't stand him in school. Everyone on the football team referred to him as the class asshole."

She hadn't known that little tidbit of information but, considering the Max she knew, it didn't surprise her. "He's changed a little since then, but I swear he still thinks the sun rises every morning just for him."

"I never understood how you two were together. He didn't seem like your type."

"Our dads are close friends. They grew up together, and our grandfathers are longtime friends too. My dad and Mr. Shelton wanted to join the families. Giselle's three years older than us. Now the age difference isn't a big deal, but back then she didn't want anything to do with a high school boy."

"You were forced to date him?" Connor asked, sounding angry on her behalf.

Her dad had never forced her to do anything but clean her bedroom and eat her vegetables with dinner. "No, but I was strongly encouraged, I guess. Our two families regularly got together when I was staying with Dad. And Dad dropped hints all the time. When Max finally asked me out, I said yes." Becca used a small tree to balance herself as she climbed. "I swear Dad and Mr. Shelton were about ready to reserve a church just before Max broke up with me. They were more upset than me. Actually, I was a little relieved when he called it quits. It meant I didn't have to."

The trail grew wider, and Connor stepped alongside her again. "I was damn glad when he did."

It was the first time either of them had referred to the short fling they'd had all those summers ago. She'd avoided it during their picnic lunch and Monday night, afraid it would bring up too many unpleasant memories. Instead, they'd talked about everything from movies and music to the places they'd traveled over the years.

Her curiosity made it impossible for her to let his comment go, though. "Really?"

"Hell yeah. All year I wished you'd dump the jerk." He stopped walking and turned toward her. "You were the hottest girl in that damn school. Trust me, all the guys wanted you—including me."

CONNOR REGISTERED the surprise and slight embarrassment on her face, but he didn't regret his words. He believed in being honest and up-front. It might make some situations uncomfortable, but it made life simpler in the long run. "And that hasn't changed," he said, stepping closer.

He'd seen the way she watched him. She might not be willing to make the first move today, but he had no problem doing it. He covered her lips with his, slowly taking his time to learn the feel of them against his. Connor kept up the gentle massage until her fingertips touched his neck. Then he teased her lips with his tongue until she opened for him. Blood thundered in his ears as her tongue tangled with his and he pulled her closer, loving the way her body aligned perfectly with his. She shifted in his embrace. The feel of her against him had the head below his belt reminding Connor exactly how long it'd been since he'd had sex.

Before he did something stupid, like make love in the middle of a hiking trail, Connor pulled back, ending their kiss. His arms, however, refused to let Becca go now that they were finally where they wanted to be. Around her.

Her sunglasses kept him from seeing her eyes, but there was no missing the erratic pulse in her neck.

"I've never kissed a man with facial hair before," Becca whispered. "I like it." Her fingertips left his neck, and she took her sunglasses off. Then she pushed his sunglasses up on his head and let her fingertips brush across his cheek. "I'm glad to see you're still honest and straightforward."

The heat from her fingers burned into his face despite the short, well-trimmed beard he'd adopted earlier in the summer. "It's always the best way to be." He grabbed her hand and pressed a kiss against her palm. "When I like something, I'll let you know. If I disagree with you, you'll know it. And when I see something I want, I go after it."

Becca's eyes gleamed with the same heat that was coursing through his body. "I agree it's the best way to be, and I'm the same way." She leaned in and pressed a whisper of a kiss on his lips. "C'mon, let's keep walking before anyone else comes along."

They hadn't passed any other hikers so far on this trail, but the visitor center had been packed. At some point, they were bound to run into other people. He didn't care if people came upon them in some intimate embrace, but Becca might. The most unusual things embarrassed women.

Connor took her hand and started walking. "So Giselle is engaged to your ex. Sylvia is married, and Kassidy lives with you."

"Well, when she's not having a slumber party with whatever random guy she's picked up," Becca said.

In school, he'd never gotten involved with Kassidy, but he'd heard the rumors about her. Although incredibly smart, she had liked to have fun. Sounded like that hadn't changed. "What are Eddy and Graham up to?" He knew it was a long shot, but a conversation about her brother and stepbrother might help get rid of the erection currently tormenting him.

As they continued, Becca gave him the 411 on her family. Unfortunately, as he'd anticipated, his physical state didn't change. By the time they took a break, he knew he'd need either a freezing shower or some time naked with Becca to get rid of the erection pressing against his zipper.

"What's your sister up to?" Becca asked, accepting the water bottle he handed her.

Until now she hadn't asked about his family, and he hadn't offered up any details. Now that she'd asked, he couldn't blow her off. Especially since she'd answered all his questions without any hesitation.

"Stephanie lives in Boston. Right now she's practicing law, but she's planning to enter local politics in the next election."

Becca twisted off the bottle's lid and took a sip. "Unless she's changed a lot since high school, I can picture her working on the Hill someday."

He nodded, then pulled out a package of dried apricots and tore it open. He offered Becca some before taking a handful. "She's about the same, only even more headstrong. Yeah, I know, hard to imagine." He loved his sister, but once she made up her mind, there was no changing it, regardless of the situation. "Our grandfather keeps trying to get her to move and take a position in his Los Angeles firm. He's offered her every incentive he can think of. She refuses. Insists she loves Boston and the East Coast."

"I don't blame her. California is nice, especially the northern part of the state, but I can't imagine living there." She nibbled on her bottom lip, her expression suggesting she was considering her next words before she spoke. "Do you see your family a lot?"

"No. I see Stephanie the most. She was down this way in March. I haven't seen Mom and Xavier since last fall." He didn't add that he hadn't talked to his mom since April, either. Unless something drastic had changed, Becca had seemed close to her family when they'd been in school. Even before the FBI carted off Dad's sorry ass, the same couldn't be said about the Anderson home. After Dad's arrest, it had simply deteriorated even more.

He prepared himself for more questions related to his family. In his experience, women like Becca liked to dig into your personal life. It was one of the reasons he usually dated women more like Candy from the pub. Women like her only wanted some fun and a good orgasm. They didn't care what kind of relationship you had with your mom, or whether you wanted a couple kids and a minivan someday.

"Since most of your family lives in New England, it's understandable you don't see them often, especially with your rather unique profession. I see Graham and Kassidy all the time because they live around here, but usually months go by between visits with anyone else." Becca took a granola bar from his backpack and tore it open. "I think it was the hardest thing for me to adjust to when I moved down from Connecticut."

She offered him the second bar in the package then ate in silence for a few minutes. He was about to ask what she'd done before going to work for Senator Lynch, when she looked in his direction. "Can I ask you something?"

Not what he wanted to hear. "Go for it."

He braced himself for a question about his good-for-nothing dad, a person he never talked about to anyone, including his sister.

"After the party at Leslie's house, I tried calling you."

Her statement transported him back, but rather than focusing on finding the Feds at his house, his mind went straight to them alone in the pool house.

"You don't have to answer," she said.

Yeah, right. Whenever someone offered up those words, they were thinking something else entirely. Whatever question she tossed out next, he'd either have to answer it or write Becca out of his life again. And that wasn't something he wanted to do.

"But why didn't you ever call me back?" Becca asked, sounding a little hurt even though they were discussing things that had taken place years ago.

Never would he admit he'd been embarrassed as hell by his father's actions. While she might understand, he refused to acknowledge some emotions. And embarrassment topped the list right along with fear. "When everything went down, I was pissed at my father. I needed to distance myself from him and everyone who knew our family well. You just got lumped in with that group. I'm sorry."

He hadn't realized it until now, but he truly was.

Becca looked off into the distance. "That makes sense." She

didn't sound angry or hurt. Instead, her tone carried a note of understanding.

Connor stuffed a handful of dried apricots into his mouth and waited for her next question. Whatever it was, he hoped it had nothing to do with his parents.

———

IT TOOK A SHITLOAD OF WILLPOWER, but he'd managed to keep his hands and lips off her for the rest of the afternoon. With Becca's town house in sight, he wasn't sure how much longer his willpower would hold out. Alone at her place, they wouldn't have to worry about others hikers stumbling upon them while he got as well acquainted with Becca as she'd let him today. And he hoped to get *very* well acquainted.

"Can you stay for a while?" She touched his thigh when he turned the engine off. She'd kept her hands to herself since their kiss too. If she hadn't, all the willpower in the world wouldn't have stopped him from slipping his hands under her T-shirt to see how well her breasts fit in his palms while kissing her until she couldn't stand on her own.

"Definitely."

No longer able to wait, he leaned across the SUV and took possession of her mouth. He didn't need to urge her lips apart. Instead, she traced his bottom lip with her tongue, turning him on more than the striptease Candy had given him the last time they'd spent time together.

When she finally pulled back and opened her door, he wasn't sure he'd be able to walk to her front door.

"Oh, man," Becca groaned as they headed up the walkway. "I thought I was in decent shape. Considering how sore my legs are right now, I need to step up my exercise routine."

He stopped her on the steps and ran his gaze over her body before meeting her eyes. "Your legs and everything else look damn perfect to me. No need to change anything."

The bright sunlight allowed him to see the slight blush spreading across her cheeks. "You're definitely good for my ego, Connor." Opening the door, she stepped inside and switched on the lights. "Next time it needs a little boost, I'm calling you."

He followed her inside. "We already established I'm always honest. Just being that way now."

"Then I'd better be honest too." She leaned into him and covered his mouth with hers before he could question her statement. When she came up for air, she took his hand and started for the stairs. "Follow me."

He didn't need to be told twice.

SIX

"I've heard people butcher that song before but never like that," Becca said as Connor turned into her driveway.

No longer satisfied by the fruit she'd brought up to the room around four o'clock, they'd dressed and driven to a nearby restaurant and pub. She often visited the place because the food was decent, and every weekend the pub had live music. Usually, the bands brought in were great, but either the manager hadn't heard this one perform before hiring them or he'd been wearing earplugs when he did. The group had attempted to cover a wide range of songs, spanning at least two decades' worth of music. A few they'd managed to pull off. Most, though, had been way out of their league.

"Someone really needs to suggest the lead singer stick with songs in his vocal range."

"More like find a new profession." Connor put the SUV in park and killed the engine.

"Perhaps. But no one wants to hear they stink at something they obviously love. And he clearly loved being up there."

"I'd rather hear the truth than make an ass of myself like he did up there."

Again, she shared his sentiment. But everyone was different.

"Can you stay a little longer or do you need to get home?" They might have spent the majority of the day together already, but she wasn't ready for him to leave yet.

He gave her the same smile he had upstairs right before he'd sent her over the edge with his lips and tongue. And although they were still both fully clothed, her body ached as if he was touching her. "As long as you want."

Her mouth suddenly drier than a desert, she opened the car door. "Then I guess you'll be here the night."

"Not a problem. I always keep extra clothes in the car for work."

Good to know it was for work, and not because he regularly spent nights in someone's bed beside his own.

Connor met her around the front of the SUV, but before he let her get any further, he gave her a taste of what she had to look forward to upstairs.

Opening the front door, she stepped inside and switched on the lights. "Any interest in some wine?" she asked. "There's nothing more relaxing than a glass of wine and a soak in the hot tub upstairs. Or we can sit out on the deck and drink it."

"Whatever you want."

Connor naked in the hot tub sounded like the best idea she'd had in a long time. "Wine and hot tub." She led him down the hall. "White or...." Her voice trailed off as she glanced around the room. "Someone has been in here," she whispered.

"How can you tell?" he asked, lowering his voice to match hers.

He hadn't been in the room today, but even if he had, he wouldn't have been able to tell. No one except her would. The room looked untouched, and when people broke into a place, they weren't usually neat about it.

"While I ate breakfast this morning, I checked my email. I left the laptop there instead of bringing it back upstairs." She pointed toward the kitchen island. "And when I came down earlier for our snack, it was still there." The only thing on the island now was the salt and pepper she'd used on her eggs.

"Maybe Kassidy brought it up for you."

"She's not around. She flew out to a conference in California. She won't be home for several days." Becca took a step closer to him, her arm bumping into his.

If someone had been in the town house, was it possible they were still there? Before she could ask him his thoughts, Connor took her hand and dropped his car keys in it. "Get in the car, lock the doors, and call the cops." He pulled her out of the room and back down the hall to the front door.

She let him lead her there without argument. When he pushed her outside, she spoke up. "Aren't you coming with me?"

"Go while I see if anyone is still inside."

"But—"

"Go."

When her feet seemed incapable of moving, he gave her slight nudge through the doorway. "Connor, please be careful."

She walked to the SUV. Once inside, she glanced back at the front door in time to see Connor close it.

———

BECCA WALKED the police officers to the door and locked it after they left, although she didn't know why she bothered. Strangers had already made their way inside and invaded her privacy as well as her underwear drawer.

"It doesn't make any sense." She'd repeated the same sentiment numerous times since she got the all clear from Connor and looked around while they waited for the police.

When criminals went through the effort of breaking into a house, didn't they take anything and everything of value? Or at least as much of it as they could carry out? Whoever had come into her home had left plenty of valuable items behind. The emerald and diamond tennis bracelet she took off last night was still sitting on her bureau, although her favorite diamond earrings and the emerald pendant she'd also left there last night were both gone. And the emerald ring and watch Mom gave her as presents were still on her nightstand. Although she needed to do a more thorough inspection, there were four rings and a pair of earrings missing from the top portion of her jewelry box, but that didn't explain why anyone would leave behind valuable items in plain sight.

Her walk through Kassidy's room had revealed the same thing. Her stepsister's jewelry box was open but, at least as far as Becca could tell anyway, not much was missing from it. Why would anyone desperate enough to break into a home leave behind items like jewelry, which could be easily stuffed in pockets and later brought to a pawnshop for cash?

"You're positive there's not more jewelry or maybe some money missing?" Connor asked. He'd stuck to her like glue ever since she walked back inside.

Becca nodded. "It's a bit of a mess upstairs and in my office, but yeah. Except for my earrings, the pendant, and the four rings, all my jewelry seems to be here. There didn't seem to be any jewelry missing from Kassidy's room, and I don't keep a lot of cash in the house. I don't think she does either."

As far as she could tell the only things besides the few pieces of jewelry missing were computer devices and anything associated with them. Heck, even the flash drive she used to keep track of her checkbook was gone from her desk drawer. Why someone would want that was beyond her. They couldn't do anything with it. The flash drive literally only contained a listing of every bill she paid and each deposit she made. There were no passwords or account numbers stored on it. She hadn't even bothered to set a password to access it because the information was so useless to anyone but her.

"And you saw the bracelet right there on the bureau and the ring on the nightstand." Along with all the panties she owned, because whoever broke in had rummaged through her underwear drawer as well as many others and tossed the stuff on the floor. At least she didn't own granny panties. Talk about embarrassing. "Criminals don't leave stuff like rings and watches behind, do they?"

"Not unless they got spooked and split before they finished grabbing everything."

Sounded like a reasonable theory, and one she hadn't considered. Unfortunately, it didn't change the fact that she now had to buy all new underwear because the idea of wearing ones some stranger had touched skeeved her out.

"Or they were looking for something specific, not just stuff that would make 'em a quick buck," he said, again bringing up a possibility she'd not thought of herself.

"Like what?"

Connor led her into the living room and sat, pulling her down next to him. "Do you keep any sensitive info on your computers? Anything someone could use against Senator Lynch? Details about a bill the public hasn't been told about yet? Info about some secret backroom deals he's involved in that his opponents might like to learn about?"

She had a laptop she used only for work-related tasks, but she didn't keep any sensitive information on it. The device with that information never left her office in D.C. "No. Besides, they took more than my work laptop."

"Yeah, but whoever broke in wouldn't have stopped to figure out which devices you use for work and which ones are for personal use."

He had a point. "My work laptop only contains information that's already public knowledge, as well as the senator's daily schedule and a few projects I'm working on. But none are a matter of national security or anything. I don't keep any sensitive material on it. I really can't see why anyone would be interested in it."

Leaning forward, he rested his elbows on his knees. "You'd be surprised who might want a United States senator's schedule." The lines of concentration deepened along his eyebrows. "What does Kassidy do for work? Is she on the Hill too?"

Well, she knew where her stepsister worked, but not exactly what she did there. "She works for Lafayette Laboratory. Something to do with developing artificial intelligence systems. Honestly, the few times she's mentioned anything about the subject my head has started to hurt. Anyway, Kassidy can't bring anything home from work. And sometimes I envy her for that. Makes doing any work-related tasks at home impossible."

"It's possible whoever was in here thinks you or Kassidy do keep sensitive information at home and hoped to get it."

Until now she'd never minded living alone. But a shiver wracked her body at the thought of being in bed and having someone creeping around downstairs. "Do you think they'll come back?"

"Doubt it. But you need to change the locks on your doors. What you've got might look nice, but they're crap. I could pick them half-asleep and be inside before you ever realized it."

His comment did nothing for the shivers coursing through her body.

"I'd feel better about you staying here tonight if you let me go buy new ones and install them for you. When I'm done, I'll help you clean up the mess the assholes left behind."

She'd take him up on both offers. "Yes, please. But I'm not sure I'll sleep here tonight." New locks or not, she might not stay here for the next couple days. "Actually, I probably won't stay here until I get some type of security system installed."

It'd been on her to-do list for a long time and yet she'd never gotten around to it because she'd always felt perfectly safe. Whoever had come in today had destroyed that.

"Do you have a place to go?"

Becca nodded. "I'll give Ted and his wife a call. They're like family. I stayed with them when I first moved down here before I closed on this place. They won't mind if I spend a few days with them."

"You're welcome to stay with me instead," Connor said. "The commute into D.C. won't be as good as it probably would be from the senator's house." He leaned closer to her and touched her cheek. "But I guarantee you, the stay will be much more pleasurable."

Connor covered her mouth with his lips, preventing her from answering—not that it was a difficult decision to make.

"As long as you don't mind," she said when he finally gave her an opportunity to speak again.

"I wouldn't have offered if I didn't want you there."

"Then it looks like you have a new roommate for the next couple days."

Connor smiled, and desire replaced the unease she'd felt since she discovered someone had been in the house and rummaged through her belongings.

"Do you want to come with me to get the new locks, or stay here and start on the mess you have?" he asked as he stood up.

Like he needed to ask. Even if some creepy stranger hadn't walked through her house and searched through her underwear drawer earlier, making her not want to be here alone, she'd take every opportunity she could to spend time with Connor. "I'll come with you."

SEVEN

DALE HAD PURCHASED the two-story brick colonial in Leesburg, or rather one of the many shell corporations he was involved with had, when he'd still been married. It didn't matter if he was meeting with a less-than-reputable business associate or his mistress when he'd still been married, the home provided him ample privacy while not requiring a long commute.

Tonight he wasn't headed out there for any type of meeting.

Regardless of when he'd last been there, Melanie came in every Monday afternoon to clean and accept any packages he had delivered there rather than to his condo. She'd worked for him since he bought the place. He trusted very few people, but he knew she'd never go to the authorities regardless of what was delivered to the house or by whom. He'd made it clear when he hired her that immigration officials would suddenly learn her husband was once again living in the United States if she ever drew attention to who or what showed up at the door.

Her husband was a former client he'd helped beat drug and weapon trafficking charges, although he'd been guilty as hell. The man, who had overstayed his visa by five years, had been deported following his trial. However, mere months after he'd been sent back to his home country, he'd reentered the United

States illegally and was once again living with his wife and their two sons. Under no circumstances did his employee want her husband sent away again.

Since Melanie would be here today, he'd instructed Zane to deliver the items retrieved from Becca and Kassidy's house this morning. The chances of the information he wanted actually being on any of the devices were slim, but worth a shot. Honestly, what he really hoped to find at this point was a lead as to where Kassidy had disappeared to. She and her stepsister lived together. Hopefully, she'd sent Becca an email or text message with her location. Even if she'd only sent a general location, Zane had enough associates across the country to find her. And once Zane got his hands on Kassidy, it'd be easy to get the information Dale wanted from her.

A nondescript cardboard box sat on the kitchen counter. Dale sliced through the packing tape keeping it closed. Inside he found three laptops, numerous thumb drives, a backup hard drive, and two tablets. There was no way to tell which, if any, of the items belonged to Kassidy and which ones belonged to her stepsister. Dale hoped none would be password protected, though. While he had a guy, another former client, who'd be able to crack almost any password either woman might have used, it'd be one more person he needed to get involved. Already he'd involved more than he was comfortable with.

Before he touched a single item, Dale slipped on a pair of latex gloves; even if the chances of anyone finding the devices later were virtually nonexistent, he saw no reason to leave his fingerprints on anything. Then he pulled out the laptops and headed back out. While he often connected to the unsecured Wi-Fi network in his neighborhood, he didn't want to use it for this. Instead, he'd drive over to the busy shopping center and access the Wi-Fi from one of the fast food restaurants there.

Ten minutes later, Dale was parked in a far corner of the center's lot. Grabbing one of the laptops off the front seat, Dale opened it and powered the device on. Immediately an icon picture of a sailboat appeared, along with a password box. Despite advice to come up with complex passwords, people still used easy-to-remember ones like their birthday or a pet's name. He didn't know if Becca or Kassidy had any pets, but thanks to public records and the internet he knew their birthdays. He typed in Kassidy's birthdate first and hit Enter. When the laptop rejected it, he tried Becca's.

A picture of the ocean filled the screen, along with at least a dozen labeled file folders. The one marked Christmas photos suggested this was Becca's personal laptop and not one she used for work.

Unable to move the cursor with the gloves on, he tore off the latex covering his right index finger and used it to move the cursor over the system preferences icon and connected to the burger joint's network. If Becca had her cell phone linked to this device, like so many other people, every text message she received would also show up on her computer now that it was connected to Wi-Fi. Dale clicked on the messages icon at the bottom of the screen. As he scanned through the recent text messages she'd received, he made sure not to touch any other part of the computer with his exposed finger. The less he touched, the less he needed to wipe down later.

Becca had a few incoming messages, but Kassidy's number —or at least neither her normal cell phone number nor the one they'd been using to communicate with recently—wasn't attached to any of them. He'd expected as much. If Kassidy was hiding or trying to avoid being found by him, she'd used a device he couldn't trace back to her. Or at least one she thought he couldn't trace back to her.

It didn't take him long to read through messages from Becca's mom and stepmom, as well as ones from her father. None of them were more than a few days old either. Unlike most people, the woman obviously deleted text messages on a regular basis. Dale reached the final few messages.

Someone broke into the house today, a message Becca sent out Saturday night read.

He scrolled to the next message. It didn't have a name or a phone number attached to it. Instead, it had a screen ID and came from a messenger app he'd heard of but never used himself. Dale didn't need a name to know the messages were between Kassidy and Becca. Who else would she be telling about a home invasion?

Are you okay?

Yes, just a little unnerved. I decided to have a security system installed.

Good idea.

They went through your things too. Not sure if they took anything.

I'll worry about it when I get home. Just so you know, I'm going to use two weeks' vacation time after the conference out here ends.

Have fun. What do you want me to do with your mail? It's piling up.

Toss it. I'm not expecting anything important. See you soon.

The messages confirmed Kassidy had been in contact with Becca but didn't give a clue as to where Kassidy was holed up. He'd check the rest of what the laptops contained and the items in the box at the house, because he had nothing to lose by doing so. If he didn't turn up something useful, he'd contact Zane again, tell him to take more aggressive actions.

EIGHT

CONNOR PULLED OPEN the door to Shooter's Pub and walked inside. Despite the joint's run-down appearance, the popular sports' pub had a steady stream of regular customers every day of the week, many of them military men and women from the nearby base. This evening was no different. He hadn't even made it to the bar yet, and already several friends had called out greetings to him. Any other evening, he would've joined them for a few beers or maybe a game or two of pool.

But not now.

Tonight he was only here to pick up the takeout order he'd called in.

"Hey cutie," Candy said, stopping him before he reached the bar. As usual, the pretty waitress was wearing a sprayed-on T-shirt with the name of the pub on the front and extra-short shorts. She'd piled her hair on top of her head and applied the perfect amount of makeup to make her dark brown eyes grab you and pull you in. "I haven't seen you in weeks." Despite the loaded tray in her hands, she moved in closer to him, her breasts brushing against his arm. "I have one table open. It's over by the windows. Go grab it, and I'll be right over."

Several months ago he would've smiled and headed for the

empty seat. Then he would've stayed until closing and taken Candy back to his place for the evening. Even if he didn't have Becca as a temporary roommate right now, he wouldn't have done so tonight. Sure, they'd had some fun together, but he had no desire to spend any more time with Candy—a fact his buddy Keith would give him hell about if he knew.

"I'm not staying. Just picking up a takeout order I called in." He took a step back, putting some space between them.

Candy pouted; there was no other word to describe her expression. "Oh, well, my shift ends at nine o'clock. I can stop by your place on my way home. Or you're welcome to meet me at mine. Either works for me." She moved in toward him again.

Connor considered his options. He knew her type. If he said not tonight, she'd interpret it to mean "let's hook up some other time." Regardless of where this thing with Becca went, he had no desire to have sex with Candy ever again. Honesty usually served him well, but telling Candy he had a girlfriend sounded like something a twelve-year-old would say. And he wasn't sure it was the truth anyway. Yeah, there was definitely something between him and Becca, but where it would lead was anyone's guess.

Stick with the truth. "I'm seeing someone." It sounded better than saying he had a girlfriend staying with him.

"Darn," she said, a true frown forming on her face this time. "Whoever she is, she's lucky." She shrugged a shoulder. "Oh well. If you're ever single again, you know where to find me. We always have fun together." Candy adjusted the tray she held. "Have a nice night." Before he answered, she walked away toward a table of twentysomething-year-olds, catching the attention of a lot of guys around him.

He watched her flirt with the blond man seated with the group, and couldn't help comparing her to the woman he'd have in his bed again tonight. While there was no denying Candy was pretty, she couldn't compete with Becca. And it might sound stupid, but Becca's beauty wasn't only about what was on the outside. She was thoughtful and kind. Since she'd been staying with him, there hadn't been an evening when she hadn't inquired about his day. Whenever he'd been with Candy, it'd all been about the physical pleasure. There had been no in-depth conversations or sharing of each other's day. He'd never considered his life lacking anything, but since Becca walked back into it, he'd started reconsidering that belief.

"Hey, Connor!" a familiar voice called out. He turned in the direction it had come from, and found Brayden Delray seated at the bar. They'd served together, but he hadn't seen the guy since the spring when Brayden's mother-in-law had last been in town.

"Brayden." He clapped the guy on the shoulder. "How's it going? Mother-in-law visiting again?" It was no secret Brayden didn't get along with his mother-in-law, and whenever she was in town, he spent as much time away from home as possible.

He nodded and reached for his beer. "Unfortunately. But she's leaving tomorrow night. So my visit to hell is almost over." He took a gulp before setting the glass down. "What about you? Alone tonight, or are you meeting someone here?"

"Just picking up dinner," Connor replied as the bartender approached. He gave the man his name and order number before turning his attention back to his friend. "How's Laurie?"

"Miserable. Sick every morning. Doc said it would get better in the second trimester, but it hasn't."

"She's pregnant?" He'd spent countless Sundays at Brayden's house, watching football. The last time he'd seen Laurie had been for a Super Bowl party they'd hosted back in February.

"Five months."

The bartender set Connor's order down and accepted the cash in his hand before walking away. "Congrats, man." He slapped Brayden on the shoulder again. "I'm happy for you both. Tell Laurie I said hello." He picked up the bag of food. "I'll stop by soon."

When he pulled into the driveway, Becca was closing her car door with her hip. She had her purse and briefcase in one hand

and two large pizza boxes in the other. When she heard his car, she spun around, almost dropping the boxes in the process. She smiled once she spotted him.

"Great minds think alike." He held up the takeout bag from the pub and crossed to her.

"Or at least hungry ones," she said, leaning closer to kiss his cheek. She nodded toward her trunk. "I picked up some wine too. It's in the trunk. I didn't think you had any."

He'd always been more of a beer drinker, but given the right circumstances, he drank wine as well. If Becca preferred wine with their dinner tonight, he wasn't going to complain. "I'll grab it." He used the key fob still in her hand to pop the trunk and pulled out the bag.

Wine and dinner from Shooter's in hand, he unlocked the front door and held it open for her. When he followed her inside, he again wondered what she thought of the place. Never before had he cared what a visitor thought of his house, but since her arrival Saturday night, the thought had crossed his mind several times. While in excellent condition, the tiny ranch-style home was close to sixty years old and lacked many of the amenities newer homes had, such as central air conditioning and an attached garage. Since he'd originally moved in as a renter, he'd assumed the place would only be temporary anyway and had overlooked the things the place was missing. When the owner decided to sell a year ago and offered it to him before contacting a real estate agent, he'd accepted immediately with the intention of updating the home when he got around to it. Somehow he still hadn't gotten to any of the changes he wanted to make. Still, the outdated home didn't bother him. It might bother a woman like Becca, though. She was used to having the best of everything, and that included where she called home. Her own house was a perfect example of that.

"I wanted to cook us dinner tonight," Becca said, interrupting his inspection of the kitchen and all the things he wanted to change about it. "By the time I left the office, there wasn't time to go shopping."

He'd dated plenty of women, but none had ever cooked for him. "Don't worry about it. It's why takeout was invented."

She left the pizzas on the small kitchen table. It had been there when he started renting the place, and the owner told him to keep it after the sale. Connor guessed the table might be as old as the house. It certainly looked like it. Unlike the home, it had definitely seen better days. Since he usually ate alone in front of the television, he rarely noticed, though. Tonight he was noticing every scratch and chip in the wood.

Becca got out two plates and added them to the table. "I'll cook for you this weekend," she promised before going back to the cabinets. "Do you have any wineglasses?"

"Sorry, no."

She took two water glasses out instead. "The alarm company will be finished at my house tomorrow. Hopefully they'll be done early. They worked until three today, and then I went to the office. I did some stuff while they were at the house, but I find it hard to concentrate with them there. Even when I'm alone at home, I tend to get distracted easily. All the noise they were making didn't help."

He'd been surprised when she told him she didn't already have some type of security system in her house. If he'd been a single woman living there, it would've been the first thing he had installed when he moved in. Becca hadn't had a good reason for why she hadn't. But Saturday, while he changed the locks on her doors, she arranged for a company to start installing one immediately. She hadn't given him a dollar amount, but she had shared that the alarm company was charging her a premium to get the job started immediately and finished quickly.

Connor hadn't expected to spend much time with her tomorrow anyway. This morning he'd taken over for Spike and was now watching over Deborah Stone, the wife of an English politician, and her daughter, who was here to not only sightsee but also look at possible universities. Unless the Stones suddenly changed their minds about attending the performance at the theater tomorrow night, he'd be with them until they returned safely to their downtown hotel room. But he had assumed he'd come home afterward and again find Becca asleep in his bed. Or at least asleep until he woke her up in the most pleasurable way he knew how, like he had last night. If the security system was up and running tomorrow, she'd probably return to her place rather than spend the night with him again.

"What did you bring home?" Becca pointed toward the bag from Shooter's. "I've never heard of that restaurant. Is it nearby?"

"About ten minutes away." Connor removed two clear plastic containers from inside. "Grabbed two grilled chicken salads. I remembered you saying you had them often for lunch because they're healthy. And I wasn't sure what else on the menu you would enjoy and would keep until you got back here tonight." He took out the last item in the bag. "I also ordered some onion rings. They have some of the best around." He opened the cardboard container and grabbed one then held it toward her. "Help yourself."

BECCA WASN'T sure where their relationship would ultimately lead, but if Connor thought enough to order her a grilled chicken salad, it had potential. She took an onion ring from the container and set it on her plate. "I think I'll save the salad for lunch tomorrow. This pizza has been calling my name since I picked it up." She opened one of the two boxes. A large pizza covered with every type of meat imaginable greeted her. "Meat lover's."

During their short involvement following graduation, they'd enjoyed more than one pizza together. Somehow she remembered he loved his topped with enough meat to clog a person's arteries.

His eyebrows went up. "You remembered." He kissed her hard and quick on the lips before taking two slices.

"And this one is a Caribbean, or at least that's what the restaurant near me calls it. I had to order it special from the place on Broadway, and they asked me to repeat myself twice. I guess they thought they'd heard wrong." She opened the second box. "Basically it's a Hawaiian pizza, but instead of ham and pineapple it's grilled chicken and pineapple."

Connor took a slice of it as well. "As long as it has a crust, I'll try it."

They ate in silence for a few minutes, but she didn't mind. While they might not be talking, she still found it nice to have someone sitting across the table from her. Even though she technically had a roommate, most nights she ate alone unless she was attending some work-related function. Even when Kassidy wasn't traveling for work or on vacation, she was rarely home for meals. In some respects, it did make life easier. She could eat what she liked and when she wanted. Before her little stay at Connor's house, she hadn't realized how much she wanted someone across the table to enjoy her meals with while discussing her day.

Well, maybe not just anyone.

The more time she spent with Connor, the more she wanted to be with him and only him. And the kitchen wasn't the only place she enjoyed having his company.

It'd taken them more than a decade to finally finish what they'd started in Leslie's pool house, but it'd been so worth the wait. Each time they had sex it was better than the time before. And afterward, Connor wrapped his arms around her and held her until they both fell asleep. When she climbed into her own bed tomorrow night, she was going to miss not only the physical pleasure she experienced with him but also falling asleep in his arms.

"I have to attend a party at Ted's house tomorrow night. I'd love it if you came with me." Some social events she could skip, but there was no getting out of this particular one.

His hand paused with his pizza inches from his mouth. "Sorry, I can't. I'll be working." Connor took a bite and chewed before speaking again. "I've been assigned to keep an eye on Deborah Stone and her daughter while they're in Washington. Spike was with them, but the poor guy is sick as a dog. He couldn't even get out of bed this morning, so Ax handed the assignment over to me. Tomorrow night they have tickets to a performance at the theater, and I have to go with them."

Even before she asked him, she knew it was a long shot he'd be able to attend on such short notice. Still, his answer disappointed her. If he had an assignment, it might mean she wouldn't see him again for several days. "How does that work? Since you're here now, you must not have to stick with them twenty-four-seven. Does that mean someone takes over for you at night? Or are they on their own?"

With another mouthful of food, he could only shake his head. After he swallowed, he said, "Depends. With some assignments, I'm with the individual around the clock. Others we work in shifts, and sometimes we only need to be with them for parts of the day. On this job, once I deliver them safely back to their hotel for the night, I'm free to do what I want. The husband only hired the firm to be with them when they're outside the hotel. Their floor requires a special access card in the elevator, and the hotel has decent security, so the guy figures they'll be safe without any additional bodies around."

"And then you go back to their hotel each morning?"

"Yep. I'll be their shadow until they board their plane back to England." He took his first bite from the Caribbean pizza, chewed, and swallowed. "Wow, this is good. When you said pineapple, I didn't have high hopes, but the combination works."

For the moment she ignored the other questions she had about his upcoming work schedule. "You've never had pineapple on pizza before?"

Even before she found the Caribbean listed on the takeout menu from the pizza place close to her, she'd frequently ordered a Hawaiian pizza, which was a staple at almost every pizza joint in the country.

"Nope. Always found the idea of pineapple on pizza odd." He washed down his food with some wine. "You're welcome to come back here after the senator's party."

As much as she loved seeing him at night and in the morning, she was almost out of clothes, and the commute was getting to be a pain. Plus, she didn't want to do anything that might put unnecessary stress on their new relationship. Overstaying your welcome at someone's house could certainly cause stress and disagreements.

"It's going to be a really late night, and my house is closer to Ted's than here."

"Makes sense. If you change your mind, just let yourself in. I don't know when I'll be home, but I'll be back at some point."

Becca sipped her wine, grateful for the invitation. Since the break-in, she'd spent very little time in the house alone. The little she had been there was during the day. She wanted to think she'd be fine alone tomorrow night, but she wasn't really sure.

"Will this assignment last long?"

"Nah, should only be a few more days. So, unless something changes, I'll be free this weekend."

Excellent. "Good. Stay with me this weekend. I can cook you the dinner I couldn't tonight, and maybe we can do something outside if the weather is nice. If it's not, I'm sure we can find some way to amuse ourselves at my house."

The heat in his gaze almost set her hair on fire. "I'm sure we can too."

NINE

Becca shivered as she crossed the living room. She didn't remember leaving the window open, but it was wide open now, allowing a cool breeze to fill the room. Maybe Kassidy had done it. Kassidy hadn't been home when she'd gone to bed last night, but perhaps she'd finally come back. Kassidy didn't usually forget things like windows, but how else would it have gotten open?

Despite her rumbling stomach, Becca made a beeline for the open window and slammed it closed. The sound echoed around her in the otherwise silent room. Later, after she ingested some caffeine, she'd check upstairs to see if Kassidy was home and remind her not to leave windows open downstairs when she went to bed.

All the lights remained off in the kitchen. Although sunlight had streamed through the windows in both her bedroom and the living room, this room was dark, much the way it appeared after sunset. Becca didn't pause to consider why. Her stomach was again loudly protesting. First she'd eat, and then she'd figure out why the sunlight wasn't shining in this room the way it should be.

More in the mood for tea than coffee this morning, she

switched on a light and set a kettle of water on the stove before going to the fridge.

Thick, muscular arms grabbed Becca around the waist, yanking her back against a solid body.

"Don't make a sound," a male voice said against her ear. The smell of the man's breath was nearly enough to knock her out. "You'll be sorry if you do."

Despite the man's warning, Becca screamed.

She bolted upright in bed and looked around.

It'd been a dream.

She was safely in her bed, not being held captive in the kitchen by some dude with really bad breath and super hairy arms. Becca rubbed both hands across her face and pulled her knees up to her chest. She'd had a similar dream not long after falling asleep last night, only in that one she'd been grabbed by the home invaders in her office instead of the kitchen. In both versions, though, she screamed and woke up before any harm could come to her. Now, like after the first nightmare, she wondered if she should've stayed with Connor longer. Maybe picking up on the unease she was suffering from at the thought of staying home alone, he'd told her she could stay as long as she needed before he left his house Wednesday morning. Becca had considered the offer. In the end, though, she'd told herself she no longer had a reason to stay since her home now had a new state-of-the-art security system that had every bell and whistle available.

Thanks to the new locks Connor had installed and the security system, she'd felt safe enough when she walked in the house following Ted's party last night. Or at least she felt safe enough when she was awake. Judging by the dreams she kept experiencing, the new alarm and locks didn't do anything for her subconscious.

"No more wasting time," she said. "There's no one hiding in the kitchen or anywhere else." If anyone had tried to get in again, the alarm would've gone off, alerting her as well as the security company monitoring the system.

Becca tossed the blankets off and stood. Work awaited her, and sitting around behind her locked bedroom door wasn't going to get her there. She paused at the alarm console mounted beside her bedroom door. From here she could do everything from turning the system on and off to seeing who stood on the front steps, thanks to the new security cameras. Similar consoles were mounted downstairs in the kitchen and in the front entryway. She'd decided to hold off on having one installed in Kassidy's room until she returned from wherever she was at the moment. Her stepsister might not want one in her bedroom, not to mention what it might do to the resale value of the home down the road.

She turned off the motion sensors in the house but kept the rest of the system activated. The last thing she wanted was to step out in the hall and have the alarm go off, disturbing the neighborhood and alerting the monitoring company.

Despite knowing it had only been a nightmare, she still held her breath as she stepped out of her bedroom. When she reached the first floor, she checked each room, starting with the living room, before entering the kitchen. All the windows and doors remained closed, just like when she'd gone up to bed last night.

Sunlight came through the windows, illuminating the room just as much as it had upstairs in her bedroom. Still, rather than set the teakettle on the stove like she had in her dream, she went for the coffee maker and switched it on. While she waited for it to brew, she bypassed the fridge and popped two slices of whole wheat bread into the toaster instead.

"Let's see if anything interesting happened last night."

Becca opened her new laptop and brought up her favorite media site. She scanned through various stories, none of which she found overly important, or interesting for that matter, while she enjoyed breakfast. When she finished, she brought up her personal email account. She didn't get any further than typing in her username and password before the doorbell chimed. Instantly, her hands froze over the keyboard and her heart rate spiked.

"Get real. Would bad guys really ring the doorbell before forcing their way in?" she said, disgusted with herself. She'd lived alone for years and never thought twice about it. Now the doorbell was freaking her out.

She checked the time before standing. The tiny clock in the top right-hand corner of the screen read seven o'clock. She didn't get many visitors, and the ones she did get never showed up this early.

The security console near the kitchen door revealed a man and a woman on the front steps. Both wore business attire, but otherwise, nothing suggested who they were or what they wanted. Although they both looked harmless, she wasn't going to simply open the door and invite them in for tea. Becca pressed the intercom. "Can I help you?"

"I'm Detective Murphy from the Alexandria police department. I'm with Detective Reed," the man answered. "We were hoping to have a word with you this morning, ma'am."

Assuming the two individuals were who he said they were, and not some con artists, why was the Alexandria police department sending people to talk to her this early in the morning?

"I'll need to see ID before I open the door." Just because they looked the part didn't mean anything. "There's a security camera on you, so you can just hold it up for me."

"Certainly. We understand," Detective Murphy answered.

She watched the man remove a wallet from his back pocket. The movement caused his jacket to shift as well, revealing the gold badge attached to his belt. Opening it, the man held up his credentials. The woman removed a similar wallet from inside her blazer and held it up for inspection as well. At least on the screen they both looked authentic.

"I'll be right there." Becca released the intercom button and then punched in her security code before heading for the front foyer.

Both individuals still had their credentials in hand when she opened the door.

"Good morning." Detective Murphy held out his credentials again. "I apologize for the interruption this morning, but we'd like to have a word with you, ma'am."

Becca glanced again at the man's identification before checking out the woman's. They looked like the real deal, as did the badges and handguns at their waists. "It's Becca, and of course. Please come in." She wasn't in the habit of letting strangers into her house, especially when she still wore pajamas, but if two police detectives stood on her steps, it must be important.

She showed them into the living room. "Would it be okay if I went upstairs to change?"

The two detectives exchanged a look. "Of course," Detective Murphy replied.

Becca hated the idea of leaving anyone alone in her living room, even police detectives. However, she hated the idea of entertaining guests while wearing pink sleep shorts and a T-shirt that read *Will run for brownies* even more.

Upstairs she pulled on the jeans she'd tossed in the laundry at some point and threw an old Georgetown University sweatshirt over her T-shirt. Neither were exactly interview appropriate, but under the circumstances both would do.

Murmured voices reached her when she hit the bottom of the staircase, but she couldn't make out any of their conversation.

"Detective Murphy, you said you have questions for me," Becca said, entering the room.

The conversation between Detective Murphy and Detective Reed came to an abrupt halt.

"Yes," Detective Murphy spoke up, giving her the impression he was the man in charge. "We understand your stepsister, Kassidy Buchanan, lives with you."

Becca took a seat in the armchair across from her visitors and nodded. "She moved in a few months ago."

"Have you seen her recently?" Detective Murphy asked.

"Could you be more specific?" What she considered recently might be ancient history to someone else.

"Within the last week or two," Detective Reed answered.

"I haven't seen Kassidy in over a week. She's been traveling for work. I believe her most recent stop was a tech conference somewhere in California, but you probably want to double-check with someone at Lafayette Laboratory. She goes to a lot of conferences, and I might have them mixed up."

"Have you received any phone calls or messages from her?" Detective Murphy asked.

"I received some texts from Kassidy on Sunday, but nothing since."

Detective Murphy jotted the information down on a small notepad he'd taken from his jacket pocket. "Did she mention where she was or when she might be back?"

She didn't care if they were from the police department. Until she knew why they were inquiring about Kassidy, she wasn't answering any more questions. "I understand you're only doing your jobs, but I'd like to know why you're asking me these questions, Detective Murphy. Has something happened to Kassidy?"

"Lafayette Laboratory contacted us because they fear Ms. Buchanan might be in danger. She was expected back there on Tuesday," he answered. "We've already verified she attended the conference you mentioned in San Diego and checked out of the hotel Sunday. However, no one has seen or heard from her since. All calls to her cell phone have gone unanswered."

Due back on Tuesday? That wasn't right. After she'd messaged Kassidy to tell her about the break-in, they'd exchanged a few short messages. In them she'd told Becca she'd worry about what might have been taken when she got home from her vacation in two weeks. She'd found Kassidy's lack of concern odd, but hadn't questioned it. After all, it was her step-sister's stuff, not hers. If Kassidy didn't care, why should she?

But the lab wouldn't have gone through the trouble of contacting the police if they weren't concerned. Was this another case of catching Kassidy in a lie, or had someone at Lafayette made an error?

"Are you certain you haven't heard from her at any time since? Maybe you have a call that went to voice mail and you haven't listened to it yet," Detective Murphy asked, interrupting her thoughts.

"Positive. Like I said, the last time I heard from her was late Sunday, and they were short messages."

"Was there anything odd about them?" Detective Murphy asked.

"No. I sent her a message on Saturday, letting her know someone had broken in. And she responded to that text. She said she'd worry about it when she came home. I haven't had any reason to try her again."

Again, Detective Murphy wrote in his pad.

"And the messages came from her cell phone?" Detective Reed inquired.

"Actually, no, it didn't come from her cell number. It came from a messenger app she has an account with and uses a lot," Becca admitted.

"Are you certain the messages were from her?" Detective Reed asked.

Becca nodded. "It's not unusual for her to send messages from her tablet instead of her cell phone. She finds typing on it easier." Becca did too, but her phone was simply more conve-nient because she always had it with her, unlike her tablet, which she usually left at home.

"Do you still have the message?" Detective Murphy asked.

In an effort to stay organized and not clog up her phone's memory, she made it a habit to delete old messages, whether they were ones she'd received or ones she'd sent. She also regularly downloaded any photos she took to her laptop so she could delete them from the device as well. "I can check."

Becca left the room and retrieved her phone. When she came back, she quickly scanned through the messages still on the device until she reached the ones Kassidy sent Sunday. According to the time stamp on them, she'd received them at eleven o'clock Eastern time. "I deleted the one I originally sent, but I have the other ones from Sunday night."

She passed the device to Detective Murphy so he could see it for himself. While he read the short messages and then jotted down the address attached to them, she wondered if she should mention Kassidy had a second cell phone. She still didn't know if it was for work or personal use, but the police might find the information helpful—especially if Kassidy really was in danger.

"Kassidy has another cell phone. Or at least she did about a month ago."

Detective Reed made another note in her notebook. "Do you have the number?"

"Sorry, no. I guessed it was for work, so I never asked for the number."

She'd rather not tell them it was just as likely her stepsister used it to contact whatever married man she was involved with this time around. Kassidy's romantic life wasn't any of their business. But if the authorities knew the phone existed, they might be able to trace it back to Kassidy somehow. At least in the movies, the police were always able to track a cell phone back to a person no matter how little information they had to go on.

She spent at least another fifteen minutes answering questions before Detective Murphy finally ended their interview.

"If you hear from Ms. Buchanan, we'd appreciate it if you'd contact us immediately." Detective Murphy handed Becca a business card. "Both my direct line and my cell phone number are on here. You can also call the station's main number and ask for me."

Detective Reed passed one to her as well. "If for some reason you can't get through to Ray, call me."

After promising she'd call them if and when Kassidy contacted her, Becca locked the door and reactivated the alarm. Rather than go up and get ready for work, though, she retrieved her cell phone from the living room. Pulling up the last message she'd received from Kassidy, she sent her stepsister a text.

Please call me ASAP. It's an EMERGENCY.

Her cell phone came to life before she stepped in the shower, but rather than a phone number or Kassidy's name, the words No Caller ID appeared on the screen. Usually, if she didn't recognize the number, she let the call go to her voice mail.

But not this morning.

Before she touched the green icon on the screen, she said a little prayer the caller was Kassidy. "Hello."

"What's up?" Kassidy asked.

Becca dropped onto the bed at the sound of her stepsister's voice. "Are you okay?"

"Of course. Better than okay. I'm currently sitting on a deck overlooking a private beach in the Caribbean, with a hunk who can give me multiple orgasms in a row. Life doesn't get much better."

"You're positive?" She didn't detect any distress in Kassidy's voice, but the police didn't show up at your house and start asking questions without a good reason.

"Yes. You should try going on vacation sometime yourself," her stepsister answered. "Why?"

"Two detectives from the Alexandria police department showed up this morning." Either Kassidy was lying to her, or the police had their facts wrong. But why would the laboratory contact the police if they didn't truly believe she was missing?

She waited for Kassidy to ask what they wanted. When she didn't, Becca spoke. "Kassidy? Are you still there?"

The sound of her sister clearing her throat came through

before she answered. "Sorry, yeah. I was wondering if I'd heard you correctly. The police were at our house today?"

"Yes, asking questions about you. They said the lab was worried you were in danger," Becca explained. "According to them, you were supposed to report back to work on Tuesday."

"More like two weeks from Tuesday I'm expected back. My supervisor's secretary must have screwed up and put the wrong dates into the system when I talked to her," Kassidy said with frustration. "Typical. I'll call and get it all straightened out."

"They said they tried calling your cell, but you didn't answer."

"It's been acting up since we got here Monday afternoon. I'm not sure if it's because of where we are or if I need to replace it. I called you with Jameson's phone because his has good reception out here."

Back the ship up a minute. Before flying to California, her stepsister had been spending her nights with someone named Bryan. "Jameson? I thought you were seeing a guy named Bryan."

"Bryan's all the way in Virginia, and I'm not there now, am I?"

Kassidy really was the female version of a playboy. Becca looked at the ceiling and dismissed the issue of who her stepsister was currently sleeping with and focused back on the reason behind her call.

Kassidy had an explanation for everything. Her supervisor's secretary could have made an error and cell phones did act up. Still, the unease she'd been experiencing since Detective Murphy opened his mouth remained.

"Maybe you should call the detectives who stopped by today and explain too. I have both their numbers." She picked up the two business cards she'd left on her nightstand when she came upstairs.

"Good idea. Give me them, and I'll call after we're finished."

Becca read off Detective Murphy's number first, because he'd seemed in charge this morning, and then Detective Reed's. "They might try sending you a text message anyway. They had me worried, so I showed them the messages you sent me the other night. They took down the screen ID and the name of the app they came from."

"Yeah. That totally makes sense. I would've done the same thing." Kassidy cleared her throat again. "Listen, I better go and get this friggin' mess straightened out before it gets any more out of hand. I'll call you soon. I really want to hear all about how things are going with Connor. Hope he's as amazing in bed as Jameson."

Becca had no idea how Jameson ranked in the sex department and didn't care, but she doubted he could out-perform Connor. However, no matter what Kassidy told her about him or the guy she was seeing closer to home, she'd never share details with her stepsister. Unlike Kassidy, she liked to keep some things private, including her sex life.

"Good luck. Hope it doesn't take you too long to get this mess corrected," Becca said. She wanted to believe Kassidy and had no concrete reason not to. Unfortunately, she couldn't dismiss the doubts floating around in her head or the fact that the police had visited her before she'd even managed her first cup of coffee. "Call or text me when you get a chance and let me know how things go."

"Will do," Kassidy promised.

Becca ended the call. Although Kassidy had said she'd call the police, Becca dialed the number listed for Detective Murphy before doing anything else.

"Detective Murphy," she said when the man answered the phone after a couple of rings, "this is Becca André."

CONNOR WENT straight from the airport to the team's

meeting room Thursday morning, glad to be walking into a morning briefing instead of another art museum, college campus, or some fancy show. While both Deborah Stone and her daughter had been pleasant enough, he hated that aspect of his job. This morning, though, he'd seen them both safely to the airport a day earlier than planned. Hopefully, whatever assignment Ax handed him next wouldn't involve visiting museums of any kind. A guy could only handle so much of that cultural bullshit.

"Hey, Coleman finally let you out of the dog house," Connor said when he saw Mad Dog seated at the table.

"I've been back since Tuesday," she answered. "But Coleman has me parked at a desk until I finish physical therapy."

"Better than parked at home." He'd done his share of desk work since coming to the firm. Usually it involved searching for leads or listening to wires. No matter the task, it beat sitting at home on your ass doing nothing.

"For a change, Connor's right," Keith said.

"Glad you two think so," she said. "I need to have some fun this weekend. Maybe see a ball game or something. Either of you have plans?"

"I'm all yours," Keith replied with a wink. "You can do whatever you want to me."

"I'm not that desperate," she drawled.

Keith placed a hand over his heart and sniffled. "How do you like that? I offer her my body and soul, and she stomps on it."

"Seriously, I heard Central Ale House has a great band playing this weekend. Do either of you want to go?"

"Count me in." Keith looked his way. "Connor?"

He heard the silent request in Keith's voice. The guy didn't want a third wheel this weekend. "Sorry, Mad Dog, you're on your own with him. I've got plans."

The meeting room door opened and Ax walked in followed

by Spike. The guy still looked like hell, but at least he was out of bed.

"Coleman got a call this morning from Lafayette Laboratory," Ax said, getting down to business before he even sat in his usual chair.

A United States-based research laboratory located in Annapolis with several branches scattered around the country, Lafayette developed some of the most state-of-the-art technology out there. Connor wondered why such an institution would be contacting the firm.

Opening his laptop, Ax continued. "One of their scientists was due back from a tech conference on Tuesday. She never showed up. No one at the lab has seen or heard from Kassidy Buchanan since she checked out of her San Diego hotel Sunday afternoon."

Connor nearly choked on the coffee he'd swallowed. "Did you say Kassidy Buchanan?"

"Yeah, do you know her?" Ax asked.

He hadn't believed the break-in at Becca's house was simply some punk looking to make a quick buck. Instead, he'd thought it was someone searching for information they thought she might have, given her position with the senator. This new intel shot some holes in his theory. Maybe someone had been searching for info they believed Kassidy had access to instead.

"Not well. We went to high school together," he said. "I saw her stepsister Wednesday."

Ax checked the information on his laptop. "Becca André or Giselle André?"

"Becca—she lives over in Alexandria with Kassidy."

"The Alexandria police sent two detectives over to speak with Becca this morning," Ax informed him. "They're supposed to be contacting the rest of Kassidy's family as well."

"Then Lafayette thinks this is more than an employee quitting without giving her two weeks' notice," Keith said as Connor digested the information Ax just delivered.

His boss nodded. "She specializes in artificial intelligence systems. The rep from Lafayette didn't go into the specifics of her projects, but we're talking the type of technology competitors both here in the United States and abroad would love to get their hands on."

"Are we assuming she's a victim or suspect?" Keith asked, voicing the question going through Connor's head.

Kassidy had always been a little quirky. He didn't see her as the type who would steal tech secrets and sell them to the highest bidder. Even if she had the right personality for such activities, she didn't need the money.

"Until we gather more info, we're assuming she's a victim. But we need to explore every angle. The police are doing the same."

"Have the police shared any information with us so far?" Connor asked.

"They're playing it close to the vest as usual. What little we have so far has either come from Lafayette or our cyber unit. They're digging into her background now," Ax admitted. "But since you know Buchanan, can you provide anything useful?"

"I've seen Kassidy only once in over fifteen years, and it was brief. But I can't see her selling tech secrets to competitors."

Of course, he couldn't picture her working in a laboratory either. Yeah, she had been class valedictorian and all, so she was damn intelligent. Yet he pictured her living a life similar to his mom's. Married to a man she may or may not love—when it came to his mom, he honestly wasn't sure on that count—while doing nothing more taxing each day than a round of golf or a manicure, followed by lunch at one of her country clubs.

"Money's a big incentive. And it wouldn't be the first time a lab rat sold their research to the highest bidder," Keith said. "Last year there was the one from Bellsouth Labs who tried to sell his research to the Chinese government."

Connor remembered. The company had suspected the scientist and contacted the FBI, who managed to stop him before any damage could be done. In that instance, the lab rat, as Keith called him, hadn't come from one of the wealthiest families in New England. Instead, he'd been a father of four who had a drug problem and a wife threatening to divorce him.

"Money has never been an issue for the Buchanan family," Connor said.

If they were working to locate Kassidy, soon everyone at the table would know everything from her birthdate to where she'd attended college. His coworkers were smart. They'd quickly realize that if he'd gone to school with her, he came from Greenwich too. From there it wouldn't take any of them long to link him to Patrick Anderson. Even if the arrest and conviction had happened well over a decade ago, people remembered him and what he'd done. Since everyone would soon know more about his background than he wanted, he might as well lay it out there now.

"The Buchanans started their first shipping company sometime in the mid-nineteenth century. They still own half the waterfront in Bridgeport and Mystic, Connecticut," he explained. "Kassidy's grandfather still runs the company. Her father, Robert Buchanan, works on Wall Street."

Everyone at the table except Ax wore surprised expressions.

"For someone you merely went to high school with, you know a lot about her," Mad Dog commented.

"It was a small school," he answered. "And my mother and her husband live near Kassidy's father and stepmother."

"Wasn't Patrick Anderson, the dude the Feds sent away for investment fraud, from Greenwich, Connecticut? Any relation, Connor?" Keith asked, putting it together quicker than he had hoped.

As much as he wished he could, he couldn't deny it. "Unfortunately, the asshole is my father."

Across the table, Spike let out a low whistle. "Someone's been keeping secrets."

"You can discuss Connor's secrets over tea and cucumber sandwiches on your own time," Ax said.

And at some point, everyone at the table except Ax, who already knew all about his past, would question him. For the moment, they had more important matters to discuss, and everyone present knew it.

"Connor, how well do you know the family? According to my intel, she has a biological sister and brother, as well as two stepsisters and a stepbrother."

He nodded. "Except for Becca, I haven't seen any of them in years. But I know her stepbrother Graham lives in the area, and her sister Sylvia is married to Benjamin Rowe, the only son of Bruce Rowe. No idea where they live." He searched his brain for any other family details Becca had shared, even though it was highly likely Ax already had the info at his fingertips. "Her stepsister Giselle André is engaged to a man named Max Shelton, and they still live in Connecticut. Her brother Edwin is currently living in London."

"Yeah, that's basically what we got so far too," Ax said. "How well do you know the stepsister she lives with? Any chance she's involved in Buchanan's disappearance?"

"Well enough." At the moment, his boss didn't need to know he was intimately involved with Becca. Depending on where the investigation went, that could change. "There's no way Becca André is involved in whatever happened to Kassidy," he answered. "Did the police pass along that someone broke into Kassidy and Becca's home over the weekend?"

"No. Do you think it's related to this situation?" Ax asked.

"Not 100 percent sure, but it didn't seem like a typical home invasion. Whoever it was left behind thousands of dollars' worth of jewelry. And some of it was in plain sight. Stuff easy to swipe and carry. But they made sure to take all the laptops, tablets, and backup hard drives in the place."

"Would've been nice for the Alexandria police to share. My gut tells me the two are connected." Ax stroked his chin, a clear sign he was deep in thought. "Get in contact with Becca André as soon as possible. I want you to get whatever you can from her. She might know something and not even realize it."

Pumping Becca for information wasn't how he'd hoped to spend his night. But Ax was correct—she might know something that could help them find Kassidy and bring her home safely. "Will do."

TEN

UNLIKE OTHER CRIMINAL activities he'd been known to engage in, he'd always found kidnapping the most exhilarating. Unlike ordering a simple drive-by shooting or getting drugs into the hands of junkies, it took a lot of planning. Not only did you have to determine the optimal time and the place to grab the person, but also you needed a safe location to stash them until you got what you wanted from them. With so many variables in play, he never left the planning to his boys. He did usually let them do the heavy lifting these days though. He'd put in his time being someone else's muscle. Now he preferred to distance himself from his organization's activities as much as possible.

Not this time.

Dale insisted the woman remain unharmed until after he used her to get what he needed. Zane didn't trust his boys with Becca André. They'd leave her breathing but not untouched. Too much money was on the line to disappoint Dale in any way. After, his boys could have their fun with her. Well, after he had his, of course. There was no way he was passing along that fine piece of ass to his boys before he had his fill.

Zane watched her approach her usual bench. He, along with a few of his most trusted employees, had been following her since the day before they broke into her place. The bitch was predictable during the day, making his job so much easier. Although he could take her from her house at night, it would mean getting her security system disabled. Thanks to his connections, he could get it done before she even realized it was offline, but he considered such a tactic his last resort.

His surveillance of her house and neighborhood showed most of her neighbors had security systems with cameras. At this point, he wasn't willing to risk getting caught on video taking Becca from the house and putting her into a van.

Besides, such a plan lacked any originality. Anyone could force their way into someone's bedroom and take them against their will. Not everyone could convince a victim to come willingly.

He could.

He'd done it before, and this afternoon he planned on doing it again.

Zane crossed the span of grass toward her. At the moment, she had her head tipped back and her eyes closed. He was only a few feet away when she looked down at the grinder he had watched her buy from a nearby food truck and started to unwrap it.

WHENEVER POSSIBLE, Becca left her office and enjoyed lunch on the National Mall. The sight of the Washington Monument looming at one end and the Lincoln Memorial at the other never grew old no matter how many times she saw it. Thankfully, there were both food trucks and fast food restaurants nearby, so she could get a quick meal and enjoy the view.

Although definitely not the healthiest of options, she grabbed an Italian sausage grinder smothered in onions and peppers after leaving the office and then headed to one of her favorite benches near the Reflecting Pool.

As expected, she wasn't the only one out enjoying the late

summer day. Tourists from around the world as well as others who called D.C. home strolled up and down the area, filling the air with a mix of accents and languages.

Tipping her head back, she closed her eyes and let the sun warm her face. When the scent of her lunch made ignoring it any longer impossible, she opened her eyes and unwrapped the belly-buster of a grinder in her lap. Biting into it, she wondered what she and Connor could do outside again this weekend. All too soon the days would be shorter and, unfortunately, chillier. Before the weather changed, she wanted to soak up as much fresh air and sun as possible, and she couldn't think of anyone she'd rather do it with.

Do it. The innocent thought brought to mind her brief conversation with Kassidy. Or, more specifically, Kassidy's comments about being with a hunk who gave her multiple orgasms in a row, which, in turn, brought up thoughts of the last time she'd been with Connor.

He'd woken her up Wednesday morning in the most pleasurable way imaginable before heading out. Since then she'd spoken to him, but unfortunately, his assignment as the Stones' bodyguard and the senator's party kept her from seeing him. Thankfully, he was supposed to deliver them to the airport this morning, so they should have the whole weekend together. For a moment, Becca closed her eyes again and envisioned him naked next to her.

"Hey," a male voice said from close by. "I hoped I'd see you here again today."

Occasionally when she sat out here for lunch, people struck up conversations with her. Impersonal and brief conversations, especially with tourists enjoying the capital for the first time she didn't mind. She hated the instances when men hit on her because she was sitting alone, and they seemed to think it was perfectly acceptable. Whoever this man was, she suspected he wasn't stopping to comment about the weather or the sight of the Washington Monument. Becca opened her eyes and glanced at the man standing near the bench and interrupting her pleasant daydream.

"Hello." She gave him a brief smile rather than telling him to get lost like she really wanted to do.

"I often see you when I stop here for lunch. This is one of my favorite spots too."

Becca didn't recognize him, but usually she preferred to take in the view rather than who might be sitting on the surrounding benches. "It's beautiful here."

"You must work nearby," the man said.

She hated to be rude, but she saw no need to tell a complete stranger where she worked. "Uh, yes. I don't work far from here."

In her experience, when she didn't encourage more conversation by asking questions, men usually got the hint and left. Hoping the same tactic would work with this guy, she looked straight ahead and took another bite of her grinder.

Her peripheral vision alerted her to the fact that, rather than walk away, her unwanted visitor sat on the bench and made himself comfortable.

"I started working for the IRS back in January. I moved here from Florida and am still finding my way around. What about you? Have you always lived around here?"

As a general rule, she tried not to judge people based on appearances. Sometimes it was difficult, though, and right now was one of those moments. Exactly what it was about the man, she couldn't say for certain. Yes, he was dressed in a suit and wore a tie, but despite his clothes and polite talk, she couldn't picture him working for the Internal Revenue Service or any other government agency.

"I've lived here for several years. It's a great city. There are always interesting things going on." She shifted her position in an attempt to put more space between them and still remain seated.

"My name's Ross, by the way. What do you say we go grab some lunch? My treat."

She didn't care what his name was. There was no way in the world she'd leave this park with him. Becca gestured toward her grinder. "I'm all set, but thank you." *Please take a hint, buddy, and get lost.*

The man moved closer on the bench, and his thigh brushed up against her leg. The slight contact set off warning bells in her head.

"C'mon, I know a great little Italian restaurant about ten minutes from here. You won't be disappointed."

If he couldn't take a hint and leave, she would. "I really don't have time for anything else today." She checked her watch. "Wow, actually it's later than I thought. I don't even have time to stay and finish this. I'll have to eat it at my desk." She wrapped her grinder back up and slipped her purse back onto her shoulder. "Have a nice afternoon."

She stood and took a step away. For the next week or so, she'd be taking all her lunch breaks safely behind her office door rather than risk running into this guy again.

"Please let me walk you back to your office." The man stood too, making the warning bells echo louder. "Like I said, I see you here all the time. I'd like to get to know you better. If you're not busy after work, let's meet for some drinks or dinner."

"I'm sorry. I have a boyfriend."

Rude or not, she didn't stick around for his reply. She walked away as quickly as possible considering her footwear. She didn't slow down, either, until she pulled open her office door.

TEN MINUTES LATER, Zane took a long drag from his cigarette. Damn bitch. Now he had to either go into the house and take her or get her as she left work. Either way, he ran the risk of getting caught on surveillance cameras because, like the houses in her neighborhood, the garage where she parked had a few cameras inside. Whichever plan he settled on, he had to decide soon. Dale Fuller didn't like to be kept waiting. Anyone else, he'd say fuck it and work on his own timetable, but keeping a man like Dale happy only benefited him and his organization in the long run.

The cell phone on the dashboard rang. There was no name on the screen, just a number. He didn't need a name to know who would greet him when he answered. *Fuck.*

He took a final drag from his cigarette before flicking it out the car window. "Yeah," he said.

"Is it done?" Dale asked.

"Not yet."

All Zane heard for several seconds was the sound of traffic. Dale always called from public places.

"Why not? You said it'd be done by the end of the week."

He didn't need to see the dude's face to know how furious he was. The rage came through in his voice.

"I made an attempt today, like I said I would. The bitch didn't take the bait."

"Do what I'm paying you for. Or I'll find someone who will. "

If anyone else spoke to him the way Dale was, he'd suffer for it and then find himself at the bottom of the Potomac. But Zane never knew when he might need Dale and his connections again, so he'd let the insult and disrespect slide.

For now.

At some point, the dude would no longer be a possible asset. Then Congressman Dale Fuller would pay for every slight he'd ever given him.

"I'll handle it," Zane said, his jaw clenched so tightly his lips barely moved.

He lit another cigarette. He knew Dale was after information and some chick named Kassidy Buchanan. It was why his boys had taken every computer device in the house while also helping themselves to some expensive jewelry. But whatever Dale wanted hadn't been on any of them, because he issued the order to grab Buchanan's roommate not long after they delivered the items. Although it didn't matter, he wondered what kind of info the guy was after.

"Be sure you do."

Just another insult Dale would pay for in the future. The dude really didn't know how close he was getting to the end of his rope. If Dale did, he sure as hell would show Zane some respect.

"I'll call you when it's done." Zane disconnected the call and took another drag from his cigarette.

ELEVEN

For perhaps the twentieth time, Becca checked her cell phone. Kassidy hadn't said when she'd contact her again, but considering their conversation this morning, she'd hoped her stepsister would call her right after she got the situation at work straightened out—assuming there really was something to straighten out.

She'd replayed the quick conversation with Kassidy several times today, and rather than go away, the suspicion that her stepsister was lying grew. Becca could understand Kassidy lying about being involved with a married man again, especially considering all the times such relationships had turned into disasters for her. But if her suspicions were correct, and there was no situation at work like Kassidy claimed, what was she hiding and why?

Becca toyed with the idea of calling Detective Murphy again. During her brief chat this morning, she let him know she'd talked to Kassidy and that her stepsister would be calling him soon. He'd thanked her for the update and told her to contact him at any time if she had any questions or concerns. Would he mind if she called and asked if he ever heard from Kassidy? She'd feel so much better if he said yes.

But what if he said no? Then what? Would that mean Kassidy really was in some kind of danger and she'd managed to act as if everything was fine this morning?

She dropped the device back into her purse. She'd give it a little longer. Calling home would be low on Kassidy's priority list if she were on vacation.

"I've been so busy I didn't even get a chance to say hello today," Danny greeted from the doorway, his presence a welcome distraction from her thoughts.

"I know what you mean. Except for a short lunch break, I spent most of my day in meetings."

"At least tomorrow is Friday, and I'm taking it and Monday as personal days. We're heading to Williamsburg in the morning for the weekend," Danny said.

Becca noticed Danny had his briefcase in one hand and his travel coffee mug in the other, suggesting he was on his way out. She glanced at the clock on her computer screen. She'd intended to stay a little later tonight so she could avoid taking any work home this weekend. However, if she left now, she could walk out with Danny rather than alone. Although she hadn't told the man from the National Mall where she worked, she was uneasy about walking through the garage alone tonight.

"Are you leaving for the night or off to a meeting?" she asked.

"Leaving. It's been one of those days, and I need to put this place behind me until next week."

"Do you mind waiting a minute so we can walk out together?"

Danny shook his head and stepped inside her office. "Of course not." Setting his travel mug on the desk, he took a seat. "Glynnis and I are meeting my sister and brother-in-law at Ellington's," he said, referring to a popular jazz club. "Join us. It'll be fun."

She'd visited the club before with various friends, although she went more for the unique atmosphere of the place than the music itself. "Thanks for the offer, but I have plans." She closed the last computer file and switched off the device.

"Not with another of Graham's friends, I hope."

Becca gathered up her belongings and came around the desk. "No. Connor and I actually went to high school together. We ran into each other a couple weeks ago. I stayed with him for a few nights when my new alarm system was being installed."

Danny followed her out of the office. "Bring him along. I could use an ally with Jordan there."

She'd met both Danny's sister and brother-in-law at a holiday gathering Danny threw two years ago. She'd gotten along well with both, but she knew Danny and his brother-in-law, Jordan, weren't big fans of each other. She got the impression there was a long story behind why they didn't get along, but she'd never asked and Danny had never shared.

"I'm pretty sure Connor doesn't enjoy jazz. But sometime soon we can get together. I think you'll get along well with him."

They kept up a steady conversation as they exited the building and entered the parking garage. When Danny opened the door to the stairwell, Becca preceded him up the steps, the ringing of her heels on the metal stairs the only sound around them.

"If you change your mind, we plan on getting there around nine tonight," Danny said as they exited on the second level.

Numerous vehicles remained in the garage, but there wasn't another soul around. Despite not seeing anyone, the hairs on her arms stood up and a chill went through her body. Automatically, she took a step closer to her coworker as they walked down the row of cars.

"Okay, I'll keep it in mind," she said.

They hadn't walked far when a sound caught Becca's attention, and she glanced around for the source. Up ahead she saw an athletically built man step from a large black SUV with tinted windows. She'd never seen him in the parking garage or her office building, but a lot of people from nearby buildings used the garage too. Her intuition, though, was telling her he didn't work nearby. Yes, he had on a suit like everyone else who worked around here, but there was something off. Much like this afternoon when Ross sat next to her, she just couldn't put her finger on what it was about the man.

Picking up her pace, she tried to keep her eyes on the man without being too obvious as she and Danny walked.

"Where's the fire?" Danny asked with a laugh, picking up his pace to keep up with her.

She saw the man take a step away from his vehicle and then stop. "Sorry, I'm anxious to get home tonight." Becca took her keys from her purse and unlocked the door, although they were still several feet from her car.

Even though Becca knew she shouldn't, she couldn't stop herself from glancing back at the man with the SUV. He'd moved away from the vehicle and seemed to be heading their way.

He could be walking toward the elevator, she reminded herself. She didn't usually use it because it was slow and, depending on the time of the day, crowded. However, she knew where the elevator was located, and to reach it the man would have to pass this way.

She eyed her car and wondered how quickly she could reach it if she needed to make a mad dash. Wearing sneakers, she could probably outrun the man and get herself safely locked inside. Becca didn't think she could manage it in her three-inch heels.

A ringing cell phone erupted from much closer than she'd like. She didn't look back to see if it belonged to the man from the SUV or if someone else was now around.

"Say hi to Glynnis and your sister." She opened the car door and got inside before Danny managed a response. Becca started the engine as Danny opened his mouth to speak.

"I will. Have a nice weekend," he said. "And don't forget, if you change your mind, we'll be at Ellington's around nine."

"You too." Becca closed and locked the door. Before backing up, she checked her rearview mirror. She saw the man slip his cell phone back into his pocket and then continue walking toward the elevator. She didn't wait to see if he actually got in it or not. She backed out and drove as fast as she dared toward the exit.

FROM THE SAFETY of the SUV's back seat, Zane watched through the heavily tinted windows as his prey drove away. After his call from Dale, he'd spent some time considering his options before scouting out the parking garage again. Thanks to the surveillance his boys had done, he knew Becca always parked on the second level, so finding her car had been easy. When Zane saw it was in enough of a blind spot that Hammer could grab her and avoid being caught on camera, he'd decided to go for it tonight and get Dale off his ass.

He'd done a quick risk assessment of the situation when he spotted her walking with a man. While he'd prefer her to be alone, the walking suit next to her didn't look like someone who could put up much of a fight, especially against Hammer. He'd seen what his boy could do with his bare hands and a knife. Hammer could easily take out the dude and grab the chick.

Unfortunately, just before Hammer made his move, Zane spotted a small group of men and women exiting the stairwell. They were too far away to help if Hammer killed the guy and carried Becca to the SUV, but they'd be able to call the authorities and give witness statements.

Eventually, the authorities would get involved. When Becca didn't show up for work, her boss would wonder why and call them. He didn't need them getting involved before he even delivered her to Dale.

A single call to Hammer had stopped him in his tracks. The

guy wasn't the sharpest tool in the shed, as his grandmother used to say about some people, but he followed orders well. He'd done just as he'd been told and kept on walking toward the elevator while Becca got in her car and drove away.

The driver side door opened, and Hammer got behind the wheel. "Do I follow her?" he asked.

Zane liked his boy's enthusiasm but dismissed the idea. She had too much of a head start, and he didn't have any idea where she was heading tonight. At least this week she'd never gone straight home once. Instead, she'd driven to a house in Dumfries after work Monday and Tuesday. On Wednesday she'd driven to an enormous four-story home in Georgetown that he later learned belonged to Senator Lynch, her boss. She could be headed to either of those two locations again, or somewhere else.

"No, we'll have to get her later," he answered, already running various other scenarios through his head. As Hammer drove out of the garage, he punched in Espanto's cell number.

"Keep eyes on her house," Zane said once he answered. "I want to know when she gets there and if anyone visits. If she leaves, let me know immediately and follow her."

Other than a few Spanish swears, he didn't know the language. But he'd been told the world *espanto* translated to ghost. The name fit the guy on the other end of the line because there wasn't anyone in his organization who could watch a person or a place and not get noticed better than him.

"Got it," Espanto replied before the line went dead.

Zane tapped his cell against his thigh. He didn't expect to find her, but he still kept an eye out for Becca's car as they trudged through the city traffic.

He had to make his next move soon. He'd gotten a look at her face in the garage. She'd been uneasy, similar to the way she'd been on the Mall this afternoon. When people got nervous like that, they became hypervigilant. They started never leaving a building alone, and in some cases hiring bodyguards to follow them around. He'd seen her house. If Becca could afford that place, she could hire a full-time bodyguard if she wanted. Hammer and several others in his organization could get rid of a walking suit like the one she'd been with tonight easily. However, a trained and armed bodyguard would make it a more difficult, but not impossible, task. He'd already wasted enough time and resources on this damn situation. He didn't want to waste anymore.

TWELVE

ALTHOUGH HE HATED GRILLING Becca to find out if she had any information that might help them track down Kassidy, he needed to. He'd tried calling her before lunch but only managed to get her voice mail. Later in the afternoon, he sent her a text message, but she'd quickly sent him back a reply, letting him know she was in another meeting and wasn't sure when she'd be done. He'd found her response odd. The police had sent detectives over this morning, so she knew Kassidy was missing. In that kind of situation people usually took time off from work. Why hadn't Becca?

Reaching her front door, he rang the bell, anxious to get some answers so he could report back to Ax.

When the door opened, thoughts of gathering intel for work disappeared. Instead, the need to pull her close and lose himself in her overwhelmed him. Dressed in shorts and a plain T-shirt, her hair hanging loose over her shoulders, she was the walking embodiment of a sex goddess. Stepping inside the house, he reached for her. Questions could wait until after he'd tasted her. Lowering his head toward hers, he covered her mouth with his.

Given the choice, he'd continue their reunion upstairs, but at the moment it wasn't an option. So after one more pass across her lips, Connor raised his mouth from hers. "I've missed you."

Considering her stepsister was missing and possibly in danger, he expected to see worry or perhaps sadness reflected in her eyes when she met his. Instead, he saw unease.

"How are you holding up?" he asked. Before he questioned her, he needed to know she was doing okay.

"I'm fine. A little stressed maybe. It was a crazy day," she answered. Taking his hand, she started down the hall. "I'm so glad tomorrow is Friday."

Fine? If his stepsister, Jill, a woman he didn't even like, went missing, he wouldn't be fine. Despite the bad blood between them, he'd be worried about her welfare and would do what he could to bring her home. There was no way Becca could be fine when the police and Elite Force security were out searching for Kassidy's whereabouts. Not unless she'd been found safe and the police had already notified Becca but not Ax.

"Sorry I couldn't talk earlier. My day was literally one meeting after another." Becca sat and folded her legs on the sofa. "Unless you really want to go out, I thought we could stay in tonight. Maybe watch a movie or something."

"Whatever you want." Putting off uncomfortable questions wouldn't make asking them any easier. Connor cleared his throat before he said, "Are you sure you're okay? Did you hear anything from the police?"

She tilted her head to one side and blinked. "The police? Regarding the break-in?"

"About Kassidy," he answered. "I know two detectives stopped by this morning."

"How do you know that?"

Fair question. "Lafayette Laboratory hired Elite Force to help find Kassidy."

"Hired Elite Force? I thought the company provided private security."

He couldn't go into everything the company did, but he could clear up this misconception.

"We do a lot of things. I'm actually part of the firm's HRT, hostile response team, and one of the things we do is locate missing people. Earlier this summer, I led the team searching for a missing little girl up in Boston." Connor took a seat next to her. "As soon as we were brought on board today, my boss contacted the Alexandria police, so I know two detectives questioned you. It's why I called earlier. I wanted to make sure you were okay and ask if you had any information that might help us find Kassidy."

Becca didn't speak, but she didn't need to. Her face told him she was trying to wrap her head around all the information he'd shared.

"But she's not missing, Connor. She's on vacation. I talked to her this morning."

Not at all the statement he'd expected. "This morning?"

She nodded. "Before I went to work."

The cyber division would know if Kassidy used her cell phone at any point today. Last he'd checked with them, it hadn't been used in over a week. "Are you sure it was her? There have been no incoming or outgoing calls to her cell phone in days."

"How do you—Never mind," she said, shaking her head. "Yes, of course it was Kassidy. She said someone made a clerical error when putting in her vacation days. She promised to call the lab and Detective Murphy from the Alexandria police department right away and get everything straightened out."

People made clerical errors all the time, but he wasn't buying Kassidy's excuse. The lab wouldn't want to spend unnecessary money searching for a person who was simply on vacation. If Kassidy had called them, someone would have reached out to Elite Force to let it know its services were no longer required, saving a lot of money.

Becca's voice said she wasn't buying it completely either. "You doubt her explanation," he said.

She nodded slowly. "I know people make mistakes, but I've caught Kassidy in a few other lies recently. And something keeps telling me she was lying today. But I don't know why she would lie about being on vacation. At least to me. I don't care what she does."

The more she talked, the more Connor's suspicions grew. They'd assumed Kassidy was a victim. It was looking more and more like she was intentionally in hiding.

"I hoped she'd call back and tell me everything was good with work and the police. But I haven't heard from her again."

"Did you check with the detective?"

"No. Honestly, I've been thinking about it, but I'm almost afraid to."

"Do it now, and I'll call my boss. Maybe he's gotten some news since I left the office."

He waited until Becca left before calling Ax. "Becca spoke with Kassidy early this morning. She gave her a story about being on vacation and the lab making a clerical error. According to Becca, Kassidy promised to call both the lab and the detective who stopped by the house."

"We both know Kassidy didn't use her cell phone," Ax said. "And if she called Lafayette or the Alexandria police, they would've let us know."

Connor watched Becca reenter the room as he listened to Ax. Kassidy hadn't done as she'd promised, Becca's face said as much.

"Make sure you get whatever number Kassidy used to contact her stepsister and get back here as soon as you can," Ax ordered. "And make sure your friend knows to contact you ASAP if she gets any other calls or messages from Kassidy."

"Will do. I gotta go."

She dropped down next to him and leaned her elbows on her thighs. "Detective Murphy said Kassidy never called him or anyone else at the police department. And the lab never contacted him to say Kassidy called in."

At least this one time, he wished he'd been wrong.

"Did your boss have any news?" She glanced his way.

For her sake, he wished Ax had had news. "Nothing yet. And if she called Lafayette, they would've reached out. They don't want to be dishing out money."

"I don't understand." She stood and paced across the area rug. "What is she really doing? Why lie about being on vacation to me? I'm not her supervisor. I don't care if she shows up at work or not." Becca paused and looked at him. "This morning the police said they were concerned she was in danger. Do you think they're right? She's a scientist, not some spy. Why would anyone want to hurt her? And if she was in some kind of danger, wouldn't she have told me so I could get her help?"

In the last ten minutes, he'd started developing his own working theory of what was going on. And if he was right, Becca wasn't going to like it. Until he knew for certain, he'd keep it to himself. "If she's being held against her will, someone might have forced her to give you that explanation this morning," he said. "If you give us the number you used to contact her, it might help us find Kassidy."

"I didn't call her."

"You said you talked to her this morning."

"I did, but she called me." Becca retook the seat she'd vacated earlier. "After the police left, I sent a text message to her tablet because Detective Murphy said she wasn't answering her phone. She doesn't have the two devices linked, and she prefers to get messages on it instead of her phone anyway. Not long after, she called me."

She ran her fingers through her hair and then down her face. "But Kassidy didn't call from her cell phone. At least not the phone I have the number for. She said it'd been acting up since they got to the beach, so she borrowed a friend's."

Connor stored away every bit of information Becca shared. Later he'd pass it along to Ax. "Then she's not alone?"

"She's with someone named Jameson. Or that's what she

told me. She's never mentioned him before, so it must be someone she either met at the tech conference or when she got wherever she is. After everything else, I'm not sure I believe her about even that. And I know several weeks ago she had a second cell phone. I heard it ringing one morning."

It didn't matter much if it was some guy's phone or a cheap, disposable one. Both could be traced. "The number should be on your phone," he said.

Even before she shook her head, he suspected she wouldn't be able to provide him with what he wanted. "It came through with no Caller ID. If I hadn't been hoping Kassidy would call me, I wouldn't have even answered it."

Another red flag went up in his head. He didn't know exactly what was going on, but it was a hell of a lot more than just a simple clerical error.

"Did she tell you where she is?" He doubted Kassidy had shared her location, but he wouldn't be doing his job if he didn't ask.

"Nothing specific. She said she was sitting on a deck over-looking a private beach and the Caribbean Ocean. But she could've lied about that too. For all I know, she might be in the middle of Kansas."

"If we have access to your phone records, the tech gods at Elite Force might still be able to trace the call and get a location." The men and women who worked in the cyber division amazed him all the time with the information they could get their hands on.

"Yeah, of course. If it helps find her, they can poke around in them all they want."

"Can you think of anything else that might help us? Maybe something she said during the call or the last time you saw her."

Becca sighed and leaned back. "I wish I could."

He did too, because so far they had very little to go on. "The people I work with are the best out there. They'll do everything they can to find her."

"Then you think she's in some kind of danger too?" she asked, biting into her bottom lip.

Either she was in danger or in hiding for some reason. "I think it's possible." He didn't want to cause Becca any additional worry, but he needed to be honest with her. "She might know something or have something someone wants."

"Do you think the break-in is somehow linked to all this?" Becca asked, voicing the same thought he'd had earlier.

"Maybe." He took hold of her hand and squeezed it. "If it is related, they took what they wanted and have no reason to come back."

ALL BECCA'S instincts had told her Kassidy was lying this morning. Her conversations with Connor and Detective Murphy confirmed it. Unfortunately, knowing her stepsister was lying didn't help explain what was going on. Connor, like the police, thought she might be in danger. But in danger from whom? Kassidy was a scientist who liked to have maybe a little too much fun, not some high-level government employee with access to top-secret information. Nothing about the situation made any sense.

"I guess you're right." Her mind went back to the encounter at lunch and the man in the parking garage.

Connor moved closer, the fabric of his jeans rubbing against her bare leg. "Has someone been hanging around?"

"No, at least I haven't seen anyone. There was just this man on the Mall today at lunch." She didn't want Connor thinking she was afraid of her own shadow. "Before you even say it, I know I'm worrying about nothing."

"What did he do?" Connor asked, his tone hard.

"Nothing really." She should've kept her big mouth shut. "He sat on the same bench while I was having lunch and said he hoped he would see me there again today."

"And?" His tone remained suspicious.

"Then he introduced himself as Ross. He said he often sees me there and then asked me to lunch." The more she considered it, the more innocent the encounter seemed. "He was just being friendly. And if he visits the Mall at lunchtime, it makes sense he might have seen me there. I go over there a lot. Besides, it's a public bench in a public park, so he wasn't breaking any laws by sitting next to me."

Connor's expression didn't change, making it difficult to guess his thoughts. "What did he do when you turned him down?"

"Offered to walk me back to my office and asked me to meet him after work." Becca shrugged. "I told him I had a boyfriend and then left. Like I said, he was just being friendly. Other men have sat down and talked to me like that while I was out there. I'm sure it happens to other women too."

"Yeah, but this one made you uncomfortable. Think about it. Was there something off about him? The tone of his voice? The way he walked? His clothes?"

Why did he have to be right? Becca ran through every detail of the encounter then shook her head. "He just looked wrong. He was wearing a suit, and said he worked at the IRS, but I can't imagine him there. But that doesn't mean anything, Connor. You can't judge a person by his looks." She considered the man in the parking garage. He'd looked out of place too.

"Still with me?" Connor asked, pulling her thoughts back to the present.

"Yeah, sorry. I was thinking about the guy in the parking garage tonight. He was parked on the same level as me, but I've never seen him around. Most of the people who use the garage work with me or in the building next door, and they park on the same level every day. It makes it easier to find your car at night. At least that's why I do it." There was nothing worse than wandering around a parking garage or lot at night, looking for your car.

She picked at the skin around her fingernail. "He could be

new. Employees come and go all the time. I'm sure I'm overreacting about him too." Normally, her imagination didn't get the better of her like it seemed to be today. Then again, the police had paid her a visit this morning before she'd even managed to shower. Considering their visit, perhaps an overactive imagination was to be expected.

"Possibly, but there was a reason he made you uneasy. Was it the way he was dressed? Did he have any odd tattoos or piercings? Something unusual about his car?"

Closing her eyes, she pictured the man again. He'd looked to be in his mid- to late-twenties. She hadn't noticed any tattoos. They would have stood out to her because the people she regularly saw in the garage never had visible tattoos. There hadn't been anything unusual about his suit except that it looked to be on the cheaper side, but not everyone could afford custom-tailored clothes. "Sorry, I can't...." Her voice trailed off, and she looked at Connor.

"What?"

"He backed into his parking space. Most people pull into them." Another detail remained just out of her reach. Rubbing her temples, she tried to think back to the very moment she first saw him. She pictured him closing his car door and starting to walk.

"His shoes." She dropped her hands into her lap. "He was wearing boots similar to those a person would wear on a worksite or hiking. Not the type a person pairs with a suit."

"And did he approach you?"

"No. He didn't speak to Danny or me. When I pulled out he was headed toward the elevator. I didn't stick around to see if he got into it."

Connor remained silent for several moments. "Until Kassidy is found, I think you should hire some protection."

"Like a bodyguard?"

She should've kept her stupid mouth shut. Just because the man had committed a fashion faux pas and paired work boots with a suit didn't mean he was dangerous. "I don't need someone following me around. I'm not in danger; my imagination is just getting the better of me."

He leaned closer and shook his head. "Maybe it is, but until this situation is straightened out, it's a good idea, Becca."

"And have everyone think I've lost my mind? No thanks. The house has an alarm, and I'm perfectly safe at work. Everyone goes through security when they come into the building."

Placing his hands on her shoulders, he rubbed his thumb back and forth across her skin. "Just think about it. Please. I'd feel better if you had someone with you."

She was touched by his concern, even if it was misplaced, but she had no intention of changing her mind. At the same time, she didn't want to argue with Connor either. "Okay, I'll think about it, but I'm not making any promises."

"Ax wants to see me." His right hand left her shoulder and moved around to the back of her neck. "I'll be back as soon as I can." Demanding lips came down hard on hers, caressing them with each pass and making it impossible to answer. Soon it was impossible to think as well.

When he pulled away, she considered asking if he'd be her bodyguard so she could enjoy similar kisses and other forms of physical pleasure whenever she wanted.

"If you need me, call." Connor stood, pulling her up with him. "And I need you to contact me right away if you hear back from Kassidy."

"Go do whatever you need to at work, I'll be fine. I don't even plan on leaving the house tonight." At the moment, she couldn't think of a single place she wanted to go except the hot tub upstairs. Hopefully, a long soak would wash away some of the anxiety eating away at her. "If she calls again, I'll let you know, but I don't think she will."

"Neither do I, but if she does, don't tell her Elite Force has been hired to find her."

If she was in danger or being held against her will, she'd want to know people like Connor were out searching for her. "Why not?"

Connor didn't immediately answer, and she didn't understand why. It seemed like a pretty straightforward question, unless he knew something he wasn't sharing. "Connor, why don't you want me to tell her?"

"We don't know who else is listening to her conversations," he answered.

Although he still hadn't said Kassidy was definitely in danger, everything about their conversation tonight made Becca think he believed it to be true.

THIRTEEN

WHEN CONNOR HAD LEFT EARLIER, she'd locked the front door and set the security system before doing anything else. Still, when she entered her room, she locked the bedroom door as well and then double-checked the console on the wall.

Yep, still on. Some might say she was a little paranoid, but having a stranger enter her home again would be bad enough. If they entered while she was naked and enjoying the jets in the hot tub, it would be a thousand times worse.

Becca crossed into the master bathroom and locked that door behind her too. Then she set her wineglass and cell phone down near the hot tub and turned on its jets.

"Turn off your brain for ten stinking minutes."

She dropped her clothes on the floor and stepped into the bubbling water. Since the moment Connor left, she'd had terrible scenarios involving Kassidy going through her mind. If she didn't shut her thoughts off for a little while, she was going to drive herself crazy.

Closing her eyes, she slipped under the water and tried to think about Connor rather than their conversation about the police and the firm. He'd sounded concerned when he suggested she hire a bodyguard. In fact, he'd said he'd feel better if she had protection until this situation ended. Should she interpret his words to mean he considered their relationship more than just a physical one?

Her own view of whatever was between them had started to shift the night they enjoyed dinner out on the deck. Since he'd called out of the blue that night, she'd thought maybe he wanted more from her than casual sex before going their separate ways for another fifteen years. So far, though, he hadn't labeled their relationship; although, in all fairness, she hadn't either. And, unfortunately, he wasn't always the easiest man to read.

When the need for air became too great, Becca popped up out of the water and reached for her wine. The moment the rich merlot hit her tongue, she wished she'd taken the time to bring a few pieces of her favorite dark chocolate up with her too. Wine and a good soak helped ease anxiety, but chocolate, wine, and a soak worked even better. To get the chocolate, she'd have to dry off and go down to the kitchen. At the moment, she didn't want to exert the effort required. She'd settle for the merlot and the hot tub's jets. Once she finished in here, she'd grab something from her stash of sweets downstairs and pair it with a second glass of wine.

She managed two sips of her drink before her ringing cell phone ruined the peace and quiet in the room. "Please be Kassidy," she muttered, squeezing her eyes shut and reaching for the device.

Neither Kassidy's name or the words No Caller ID greeted her when she checked the screen. Instead, the name Graham stared back at her. It had been days since she'd last talked to her brother. She wondered if the police had contacted him too. If they had, it might be why he was calling now. Either that or he wanted to set her up with another from his endless supply of single friends. Even if Connor wasn't in her life, she'd tell her brother to play Cupid with someone else.

"Can you come and pick me up? I'm in the emergency room at Washington General," he said after they exchanged greetings.

At the mention of the emergency room, Becca stood up and stepped out of the hot tub. Water dripped off her and puddled on the floor as she reached for a bath towel. "What happened? Are you okay?"

"For the most part, I'm fine. Just needed some stitches, but my car is totaled. Do you mind picking me up and driving me home?"

Becca wrapped the towel around her body. "Of course. I'll be right there," she said, already out of the bathroom. "Do you need me to bring anything?"

"No. I just need the ride. Tomorrow I'll work on getting a rental from the insurance company."

She pulled out shorts and tossed them on her bed. "See you soon."

Her hair resembled a drowned animal, but she didn't care. After tying her sneakers, she left the house.

Thanks to normal rush hour traffic being over and a heavy foot on the gas pedal, she pulled into one of the hospital's parking garages thirty minutes later. It took a little searching, but eventually, she found an empty spot on the third level. The memory of the man in her work parking garage popped up as she slammed her door shut.

"He was a bad dresser but harmless. Get inside. Graham needs you."

A glass-enclosed bridge connected the second level of the garage to the hospital. So rather than stand around and wait for the elevator, she headed for the stairwell. If Graham wasn't up to walking, he could wait at the hospital's front entrance while she drove around and picked him up.

"He'd better be okay." Graham had said he only needed a few stitches, but he'd been known to understate his injuries. She wouldn't put it past him to tell her what he thought she wanted to hear. "If he's seriously hurt, he's coming—"

An arm grabbed her around the waist, pinning one of her arms to her side, and her feet froze.

"Keep your *boca* shut," a voice laced with an accent she couldn't quite place whispered against her ear. But she remembered enough from high school Spanish class to know he'd mixed a Spanish word in with his English.

A scream welled up in her throat despite his warnings. Before she could let it out, a large hand covered her mouth.

The owner of the hand pulled her back against him like the intruder had done in all the nightmares she'd had. "We're going to take a little drive together, *princesa*."

Becca's heart raced, nearly exploding in her chest, and she glanced around. There wasn't a single person around to help. But if she could get to the second level and the bridge, there might be.

The man holding her took a step back. Immediately, Becca dropped her body into almost a squat like she'd been instructed in her women's self-defense class. Supposedly the position made it harder for an attacker to move you around. She prayed it helped now, because she was on her own.

"Don't make this hard and you won't get hurt." The creep tried to jerk her back upright.

Yeah right, buddy. Before he tried pulling her along with him again, she sank her teeth into his palm. When he jerked his hand away, she reached her free arm behind her and grabbed. Becca squeezed for all she was worth and slammed her heel into his shin.

"You bitch," the creep snarled, gasping in pain.

For a brief moment, the arm around her body loosened and Becca bolted.

She didn't look to see if anyone was following her. She didn't have to. She could hear the creep's heavy breathing and footsteps behind her.

Somehow she made it to the stairwell door without getting caught. Pushing it open, she ran down the metal steps, expecting that at any moment an arm would yank her off her feet and carry her back up.

Please don't let me break anything. She jumped down the last three steps. Stumbling a little, she shoved her body against the door and half fell onto the other side.

Becca ignored the stares as she sprinted across the glass bridge connecting the garage to the hospital and hopefully to safety.

"Security." Barely able to breathe, she leaned into the hospital's reception desk. "I need," she paused and tried to take in a decent breath, "security." She gasped out the word again. "Someone attacked me."

"You were attacked?" The hospital employee gave her a skeptical look, but she reached for the phone.

Taking a deep breath, Becca nodded. "In the garage. Please. I need security." She looked over her shoulder. She hadn't seen who grabbed her, but no one around her jumped out as the likely culprit.

"DAMN IT." Connor stood so quickly his chair toppled over. The sound of it hitting the floor had everyone turning their attention his way. "Are you okay?"

He shoved a hand through his hair and mentally cursed. He hadn't wanted to leave her earlier. Since she'd claimed a soak in the hot tub was her only plan while he was gone, he'd decided she'd be fine until he got back. Rather than leave her alone, he should've taken her with him tonight. Ax might have insisted Becca stay on the main level in one of the rooms reserved for meetings with clients, but at least she would've been safe. Instead, he'd left her unprotected, and she'd nearly been abducted.

But she wasn't. The reminder did nothing to ease the anger and fear buzzing around inside him. Anger not only directed at himself but at whoever had tried to hurt her. Anger he could manage. He didn't know how to deal with the damn fear. The useless emotion had never plagued him. At the moment, it was making up for missed time.

"Who's with you?" he asked before she managed to answer his previous question.

"I'm sitting in the security office with a hospital police officer. There are two officers from the metro police here too, as well as Graham." Becca's voice shook just enough for him to notice. Considering what she'd experienced, she seemed to be holding it together well.

He didn't know what kind of condition Graham was in. He only knew Becca's brother had been in a car accident, and she'd gone to the hospital to pick him up. He may or may not be able to protect Becca. Uniformed officers might deter whoever had tried to grab her as long as she stayed put. If she entered the garage, the dude might try again. And this time he might have reinforcements with him.

"Can you come pick us up?"

Like she needed to ask. He'd already pulled his keys out. "Stay put. Don't go anywhere alone. Not even the restroom."

Connor righted his chair and headed straight for Ax's office. "Got to go."

Ax's head shot up. "What happened?"

"Someone tried to abduct Becca outside Washington General."

His boss stood and came around the desk. "Is she okay?"

He hadn't given her a chance to answer that question. Since she'd called him, Connor assumed she was physically fine. Her mental state was something else entirely, but he'd deal with it later. "Yeah, but scared."

"Bring her back here as soon as possible."

"You think this is tied to Kassidy's disappearance?" Ax wouldn't tell him to bring Becca back otherwise.

Leaning against the desk, Ax crossed his arms and nodded. "I was about to give the team an update. I'll fill you in on the details when you get back."

He'd wasted enough time talking. Any other info could wait until he had Becca safely by his side.

The likelihood that whoever had tried to grab Becca sat inside the hospital's main atrium was slim. Regardless, Connor checked out every individual he passed as he crossed toward the reception desk. Not a single person sent up any red flags.

He stopped at the desk and angled his body so he could watch the building's main entrance. "I'm looking for the security office."

The silver-haired granny ran a critical eye over him before she spoke. "We had a little incident earlier."

Little? A possible kidnapping was a hell of a lot more than a little incident. Connor guessed she was trying not to worry visitors.

"Security wants me to ask for identification before calling them. Then they will come and escort any visitors down to the office," the granny continued, in a voice that could lull a crying baby to sleep.

The precaution was warranted, even if it did slow him down. Connor pulled out his driver's license and handed it over.

She looked at the identification and glanced at him before she handed it back. "Officer McGregor said you'd be arriving. One moment please." She picked up the phone and dialed. "Mr. Anderson is here."

When Becca said a hospital police officer was with her, he'd hoped the dude and the ones from metro were seasoned cops with bulging biceps. He didn't know about the ones who remained with her, but the cop before him didn't look like she could stop a mouse.

"Officer McGregor," the petite uniformed officer, who couldn't possibly be a day over twenty-four, said. "I'll bring you down to the security office, Mr. Anderson."

No one, not even his accountant, called him Mr. Anderson. "It's Connor. And thank you."

He followed the young officer down a maze of halls. Despite

not being on a floor that contained any patient or treatment rooms, the air around him still reeked of hospital. He didn't know why, but every hospital he'd ever been in smelled the same. A weird combination of industrial cleaner, concern, and death clung to them all.

Using her security badge, Officer McGregor entered the office and then led him across to a door marked Conference Room. He found Becca, her brother, and two uniformed police officers who fit the bill of what he wanted around Becca seated at the table.

"Wish it was under different circumstances, but it's nice to see you," Graham said after each of the officers introduced themselves. He stood to shake Connor's hand.

Graham had numerous bruises and scratches on his face and arms, as well as a bandage covering a section of his forehead. Otherwise, he appeared in decent shape, considering he'd been in a car accident.

"Yeah, you too." He moved past Graham and around the table to Becca. She had no visible marks, but her eyes revealed the hell she'd gone through.

He wanted to yank her into his arms and hold her. Instead, he crouched in front of her and put a hand on either side of her waist. "How are you?"

"I've been better." Her voice didn't reveal the emotions churning inside her, but the trembling hands in her lap did. "Thanks for coming."

"Anytime, anywhere." He cleared his throat as another emotion replaced the fear clawing through his gut. "And for the foreseeable future, I'll be your shadow." He didn't care if she wanted full-time protection or not. After what happened tonight, he wasn't letting her out of his sight.

Rather than disagree, she nodded—a response he welcomed because he hadn't been looking forward to arguing with her. Especially since, in the end, she'd lose anyway. Some fights he'd concede. This wasn't one of them.

Connor looked back at the room's other occupants. "Is it okay for them to leave?" The sooner he got her brother home, the sooner he'd have her safely back at Elite Force, protected by all the security measures they employed.

The cop who had introduced himself as Sergeant Holderson answered, "They're free to go. If we locate a suspect, we'll call. We'll need her to come to the station for identification."

"If you need Becca, I'll bring her down, Sergeant."

He held her hand as the three of them followed Officer McGregor back through the hospital maze and into the busy atrium. He waited until the officer left them before speaking. "Ax wants you to come back to Elite Force with me."

"As in the security firm?" Graham asked, sounding surprised. "Do you work for them?"

Evidently, Becca hadn't told her brother much, if anything, about him. But now wasn't the time for catching up. "Yeah. I was there when Becca called me," Connor answered. "Ax will have someone pick up your car later." The cost of keeping the vehicle in the garage overnight would be pricey, but it beat jeopardizing her safety.

"I've got a better idea," Graham said. "Give me the keys and I'll drive it to my house. When Becca gets around to it, she can pick it up there."

She looked at him. "What do you think, Connor?"

"Up to you." *But you're sure as hell not getting behind the wheel.* In his experience, women didn't like being told what to do. "But I don't like the idea. Whoever went after you might be looking for your car. If Graham leaves in it, he might be in danger." He paused so his words could soak in before he continued. "It'd be safer to leave it here. We can drop Graham off at home before we go to the firm."

"What do you think, Graham?"

"If Connor thinks it'd be better to leave the car, then we'll leave it."

Connor flanked her on the right, so his right hand remained

unobstructed in case he needed to grab the 9mm holstered under his shirt. Graham closed in on her left as they exited the elevator on the garage's third level. They passed a few individuals, but none did any more than cast a quick glance in their direction before going about their business.

He continued scanning the area as Becca and Graham spoke. Nothing Connor saw concerned him, but he kept his senses on high alert. There were too many damn blind spots in the garage.

They stopped alongside her car long enough for her to retrieve her sunglasses.

"I'm on this level too." He kept his left hand locked around hers as they walked over several rows. Once he had her safely locked in his SUV, he cast another look around as he crossed in front of the vehicle. The area appeared empty of people, but from his experience, there was often more around you than you could see. The sooner he got them away from here, the easier he'd breathe.

With the traffic light, or about as light as it ever got in the city, it didn't take them long to reach Graham's home.

"Get some rest," Becca called through her open window after her brother exited the vehicle.

"I will." Graham kissed her on the cheek. "It looks like Connor has you well covered, but if you need me for anything, call. I don't care about the time."

Connor waited until Graham entered his house before backing out of the driveway.

"Ax has new information about Kassidy." Instead of talking, he wanted to lean across the SUV and kiss her. Until he got her somewhere safe, he needed to keep his attention focused on their surroundings.

"Has she been located?" She sounded too damn optimistic.

He hated to kill her hope, but he doubted it was the update Ax planned to deliver. If Becca's stepsister had been found, his boss would've told him before Connor rushed out.

"Don't know the specifics. Ax was about to give the team an

update when I told him I needed to get you." He checked the rearview mirror again as he turned right. It didn't appear as if anyone was following them, but it'd be foolish not to keep an eye out for anything suspicious. "But I don't think so. He would've told me so I could pass along the news to you."

FOURTEEN

A TEN-FOOT WROUGHT-IRON fence surrounded the building housing Elite Force Security as well as the firm's parking lots. Security cameras were posted along the perimeter of the fence, recording everything that went on in and around the premises. An armed guard resided in the gatehouse just outside the fence during business hours. He or she checked the identification of each visitor before allowing them access to the visitor parking area. Once inside, security guards again greeted all guests. As far as Connor knew, not a single individual had ever made it inside the building unless he or she was expected. He couldn't think of a safer place to bring Becca tonight.

"So, this is what the home of Elite Force looks like." Since leaving the hospital, she hadn't said much, and he hadn't pushed. Everyone processed traumatic experiences differently. She might need time to work through it in her mind before reaching out for support.

Connor passed the gatehouse and turned the corner. Employees had their own entrance and parking area. "Now. They built this building twelve years ago when they developed the Hostile Response Team."

He stopped at the employee entrance and punched in his

personal access code. Everyone who worked at the firm had their own unique code. When the gates slid open, he drove through.

"It looks like this place has better security than the U.S. Capitol."

He'd never entered the Capitol building, but he'd passed by it, and he had to agree.

"Seems like overkill for a company that offers personal protection and finds missing people," she commented.

Connor parked and killed the engine. "We get visited by a lot of high-profile clients. Government officials will occasionally stop by too."

What else could he say? He didn't have the green light to tell her they also carried out covert operations for the government and sometimes worked alongside the best special ops teams the military had.

"I've heard about the firm's reputation, so I can imagine the clients who have come through." She opened her door but didn't exit the vehicle. "I'm not sure I want to go in and hear what your boss has to say."

"The team might have found a promising lead." Ax wanted him back ASAP, but he wasn't going to rush Becca. If she needed a minute to talk, he'd give it to her.

"Or he's going to tell me they suspect she's dead in a ditch somewhere."

He couldn't dismiss the possibility and wasn't going to lie. "Better to know either way."

She sighed and picked up her wristlet from the floor. "I guess we should go and get this over with, because not hearing isn't going to change the facts."

My thoughts exactly. He met her around the front of the SUV and took her hand. Although behind the security fence, he kept up a quick pace as they crossed the parking lot. A fence could keep a person from grabbing Becca, but it wouldn't stop a bullet if someone fired in her direction. Since he didn't know for certain the reason someone wanted her, he couldn't rule out the possibility that someone might try to kill her.

At the building's side entrance, he typed in his access code.

His first instinct was to take the elevator up to the fourth floor and Ax's office. As they waited for the elevator to reach them, he reconsidered. Few nonemployees were allowed up there. In fact, even some of the firm's employees didn't have access to the floor. Ax might want to meet with Becca in one of the meeting rooms on this level.

The doors opened, but instead of walking inside, he pulled out his cell phone.

"Do you want to meet us downstairs or should we come up?" he asked after Ax answered.

"Come up."

Shit. If Ax was allowing her upstairs, whatever update he had wasn't good.

Becca pointed to the unmarked door on her left when they stepped off the elevator. "What's through there?"

"Our cyber division. I don't know how they do what they do, but the people in there are geniuses." Connor pulled open the door to HRT's half of the floor.

Ax sat behind his desk, barking out orders to whoever was on the other end of the phone. When he saw Connor and Becca at his door, he gestured for them to enter. "Do that." After ending the call, he stood. "Let's use the team meeting room." He came around the desk and stopped near Becca. "Ax Germaine." He held his hand out. "Wish we were meeting under different circumstances, Ms. André."

As she reached for Ax's hand, anyone nearby would've noticed how her hand shook. "I'd prefer if you called me Becca."

Ax cracked half a smile, an event that rarely happened. "Will do." He sounded pleased, and Connor wasn't surprised.

Many of the clients who hired the firm and traveled in Becca's social circles walked into the joint expecting preferential treatment. They all but forbade employees from using their first names. Becca's statement told Ax she wasn't like her society counterparts, something he could've told Ax if he'd asked.

"Did Connor tell you why he brought you back here?" His boss walked alongside them as they headed for the team meeting room.

"He mentioned you had an update on Kassidy."

"We do, and I'm hoping you can answer a few questions that might help us."

"Of course." She squeezed Connor's hand, and he returned the gesture.

When they reached the team meeting room, Ax opened the door and glanced at him. "Get Keith. He's working as our liaison with Lafayette Labs."

He hated to leave her, but when Ax gave a command, you carried it out.

Connor nodded. "Be right back." He squeezed her hand again and dropped a kiss on her cheek. He didn't care if his boss stood only feet away.

SHE DIDN'T KNOW what Connor's boss had done before coming to Elite Force, but she was glad Ax Germaine worked for the good guys. Several inches taller than Connor, the man was built like a heavyweight boxer. A faded scar ran from the corner of his left eyebrow to his jaw. She didn't need a demonstration to know he could probably snap a person's neck with the two giant paws masquerading as hands.

"Please have a seat." Ax moved to the chair at the head of the long table.

Even though his words were polite, it still sounded as if he was giving her a command. She'd bet her newest pair of Prada heels the man had spent a good portion of his adult life in the military, barking out orders.

I'm sitting because it's the practical thing to do, not because he told me to, she thought as she complied.

"In case Connor didn't tell you, Lafayette Laboratory contacted us this morning," he said while they waited for Connor to return with his coworker.

Becca cleared her throat and shot a quick glance toward the doorway. Whatever part of the floor Connor had wandered off to, she couldn't see him. "Yes, he told me earlier tonight." Had it really only been hours ago they'd been sitting in her living room having that discussion? It felt more like weeks ago.

"Since then the FBI, the DOD, and OSI have also become involved."

Well, the Alexandria police and a special division of Elite Force Security was already involved, so why not pull in another group or two? The more the merrier, right?

She massaged her temples and hoped it would keep the headache brewing at bay until she at least got home. If not, she hoped Connor kept a large bottle of ibuprofen in his desk, assuming he even had a desk. If not, maybe there was a first aid kit somewhere on the floor that contained some.

Connor took the seat next to her before she could ask why the DOD and OSI had become involved. She could understand the FBI's involvement. They often worked on missing person cases. The Department of Defense and the Air Force's Office of Special Investigations were another matter.

Even with two other people in the room, Connor laid his hand over hers on the table. When he did, there was no missing the look the man who'd walked in with him shot Connor's way.

"Becca, meet Keith." He tilted his chin toward the fourth member of the little group. "Keith, this is Becca."

Keith was about their age, and she imagined he regularly caught the attention of the opposite sex. He was built much like Connor; she didn't need to see Keith's résumé to know that anyone who went up against him would be sorry. And, like

Connor, he carried himself in such a way that suggested he could take care of himself and anyone else around him.

"Earlier cyber discovered that for the past five months Kassidy has been making frequent withdrawals from her bank account." Ax didn't waste any time getting down to business.

Bank account withdrawals didn't seem like a big deal to her. On occasion, she stopped at an ATM more than once in a week to withdraw a hundred dollars or so.

"They range in amounts. Some have been as low as three hundred dollars, but others have been for over a thousand," Ax continued.

Okay, she'd admit that was a little odd. If you were purchasing items for such amounts, it'd be much easier to use your debit or credit card rather than carry around the cash. She actually preferred not to carry too much. In fact, usually her wallet had less than two hundred dollars in it.

"They've been made at various ATMs as well as from inside multiple First U.S. National Bank branches around this area and in a couple other states." Ax went on before anyone could ask questions. "All the locations correspond to places she has recently traveled to, so we have no reason to believe she didn't make those withdrawals herself."

Becca searched for a plausible explanation. She got zilch.

"People usually only do that for a few reasons," Keith added. She hoped he planned to share those reasons, because she couldn't come up with even some far-fetched ones.

Evidently, Ax either knew what reasons Keith was referring to or had a few ideas of his own, because he said, "Does your stepsister have a drug problem?"

The guy could've asked if Kassidy had a third eye in the back of her head, and she would've been just as surprised by the question. "Drugs?"

"People using need cash. Considering how often she makes withdrawals, it fits the pattern," Keith answered.

True drug dealers didn't accept credit cards or personal

checks, but she still couldn't believe the man had immediately gone to Kassidy being an addict to explain the money. But maybe she was being biased. She'd known Kassidy a long time, while Connor's coworkers had never met her.

"Since you know what type of work she does, you probably think she's a nerd who reads technical journals for entertainment. She's actually just the opposite. Kassidy likes to have fun," she said, wondering how best to explain without making it sound like her stepsister was a slut. "She tends to date a lot and loves visiting nightclubs on the weekend, but she'd never do drugs. She doesn't even drink alcohol unless it's a special occasion, like a wedding or maybe a New Year's Eve party."

"We didn't think drugs were the reason for her withdrawals but had to ask," Ax admitted.

Then what did they think was the reason? And why weren't they getting to the point?

"When people intend to go off the grid, they often make withdrawals like Kassidy did," Connor explained, entering into the discussion. Evidently, he knew what reasons Keith had been thinking of too. "Most ATM cards have a maximum amount you're able to withdraw at one time. And going into a bank and making an unusually large withdrawal might catch someone's attention."

Go off the grid? Had she stepped into a spy film or novel? The people she came in contact with on a daily basis didn't say things like that. "Exactly what do you mean 'off the grid'?" Maybe what she thought it meant and what Connor really intended were two different things.

Connor squeezed her hand. The gesture told her she wasn't going to like his answer. "Just what you think. Purchases made using a credit card leave a trail. If Kassidy wanted to lie low, the two first steps would be ditching her cell phone because it can be tracked and using cash for everything—from buying a coffee to paying for a cheap motel room. Getting a fake ID would also go a long way to staying undetected."

"If she got one while in a state like California, it wouldn't be difficult—especially if she managed to steal someone's identity," Keith said.

First, they were talking about going off the grid, now they were discussing fake IDs and stealing another person's identity. She really had left her normal world behind. Biting down on the inside of her cheek, she focused on the half-dozen questions floating around in her head. After a moment, she settled on the most pressing one. "And you think she's hiding or trying to stay off the grid because she's in danger?" She looked at each man seated at the table and waited for an answer.

"It's still a possibility," Ax answered.

The unspoken *but* echoed around the room.

"Becca, how much do you know about what your stepsister does at Lafayette Laboratory?" Ax asked.

"I know she works with artificial intelligence, but she never shared specific project details. And I never asked."

Connor's boss folded his hands on the table. "She's actually the project leader developing technology intended for the military, specifically the Air Force."

Well, he knew more than she did, and that explained why the DOD and the Air Force Office of Special Investigations had also become involved.

"Tonight, security at Lafayette discovered that before Kassidy left for her most recent tech conference, the computers in her department were powered off at a time when no one should've been in the lab," Keith said. "It went unnoticed because no one there was looking for any unusual activity until now. They were able to check the logs. The only employee access card used during that time was Kassidy's. She might be the project leader, but she shouldn't have been in there either."

It was odd how she could hear and understand the words coming from Keith's mouth, yet at the same time struggled to wrap her brain around them. "Maybe I missed something; are you saying Kassidy is responsible for the shutdown?"

"Details about the project are restricted," Keith answered. "The files would be too big to email out, and accessing them remotely would be impossible even for the best hackers in the world. It would be easy for a person with access to the lab to power off their computer where it's stored, remove the hard drive, and make a forensic copy of it. The lab contains the equipment necessary to do that. Once he or she was done, they could return the original hard drive, turn the system back on, then leave with the duplicate drive. No one would ever detect a copy had been made, and since nothing would be missing, no red flags would go up."

"Did Kassidy access any other parts of the facility?" Connor asked, voicing the question she had too.

Keith nodded. "She has access too much of the building. Records show that the same night the computers in her department were powered off, she entered one of the labs that contains the tech needed to copy a hard drive."

"Could she have been forced?" Kassidy loved her position with the world-renowned laboratory. She wouldn't do anything to jeopardize it. "Or maybe someone stole her access card and used it."

Kassidy couldn't be the only one working on the military project. Maybe a coworker got their hands on her card and used it rather than their own to cover their tracks. It would be the most logical thing to do if someone wanted to steal critical information and not get caught.

"When this intel came to light, security checked their surveillance videos. Kassidy entered and left her lab alone. Security also verified that no other access cards were used anywhere else in the building at that time."

Keith's answer wasn't what she wanted to hear, but Becca wasn't ready to accept her stepsister was some kind of criminal who stole secret military research. "That still doesn't mean she wasn't forced to steal whatever project information you think she took."

In movies, the bad guys often forced others to steal information or lie for them. She saw no reason it couldn't be what had happened here. But if it had, a whole new group of questions needed to be answered, including who knew Kassidy well enough to know what she did and then be able to force her to do something illegal.

Before anyone responded, the three men exchanged another look she couldn't decipher. She wished they'd stop doing that, because she hated being out of the loop, especially since it concerned a member of her family.

"You're right, Becca. And we haven't dismissed it as a possibility," Ax said, stepping back into the conversation. "But I've got to be honest with you. The evidence so far doesn't point toward her being forced."

She'd known Ax was going to say something along those lines, but she still had a hard time accepting it.

"Any luck getting a possible location using the text messages Kassidy sent or her phone call to Becca this morning?" Connor asked.

"Not yet. She used apps anyone can purchase and download to a tablet or cell phone. Both make tracing any outgoing info much more difficult. The FBI is working to get access to the data from the companies. Unfortunately, it takes time. Our cyber division is working on the problem as well."

He hadn't said it, but she could read between the lines. While the FBI tried to get access through the legal channels, the cyber division was working to hack its way into the company data. Under different circumstances, she'd have a problem with what the firm was attempting to do, but all things considered, she didn't care who uncovered Kassidy's location. She just wanted her stepsister found and brought back home safely.

She might not want to come home. Criminals went out of their way to avoid capture, and if Ax was right, Kassidy had decided she no longer wanted to play by the rules.

"You've been living with your stepsister for several months."

She hoped Ax knew about her living arrangements because Connor had told him, and not because he'd been picking through her personal information too. "Can you think of anyone who might be helping her? Staying off the grid is almost impossible, even with large amounts of cash on hand. If you have help, it's slightly more doable."

Despite the months they'd shared a house, she'd never met any of Kassidy's friends, never mind any of the men she dated. "Sorry, no. When we lived in Connecticut, we had some of the same acquaintances, but as far as I know, she hasn't stayed in contact with any of them. I can give you a list of them if you think it might help." She wouldn't be surprised if they didn't already have at least a partial list of people from Kassidy's past. "And since she's lived with me, she hasn't brought any friends over, and I never went out with her."

"What about the men she dated? Any names you can remember?" Ax asked.

"During our conversation today, she mentioned a Jameson. She said she was calling from his phone. Before she left for the last conference, she was spending time with Bryan, but she didn't give me a last name." *Assuming there really was a Bryan.* Considering all the other lies she caught Kassidy in, it was very possible Bryan didn't exist.

Becca searched her brain for more usual information. Elite Force might be the best, but assuming Bryan and Jameson were real, even they needed more than first names to go on. "About a year ago, she was involved with Congressman Dale Fuller. They were only together a few months, I think. Although with Kassidy it's hard to tell sometimes. It's not uncommon for her to have on again/off again relationships. And she was involved with Steven Levine last fall. But she hasn't mentioned either in a long time."

"Should be easy to verify when she was last in contact with both of them," Keith said.

"I can't force you, but considering what happened tonight, I suggest you hire personal protection until this situation is resolved," Ax said, more or less answering a question she'd wanted to pose but had been reluctant to do.

Becca swallowed and wished she had some water. "Then you believe what happened in the parking garage tonight is related to Kassidy's disappearance?"

"As well as the break-in at your house." Ax leaned forward and met her gaze. Despite his take-charge macho persona, she saw genuine concern in his eyes. "My theory is that someone wants to either use you to get to Kassidy and the data, or they think you have access to the research she took. Either way, I don't think you're safe alone. But you're free to do what you want."

When it came to most things, she'd agree. Not on this one. Whether she liked it or not, after what happened at the hospital, she had no choice but to hire some personal protection. Thankfully she sat inside one of the best security firms in the world. "It's not what I want, but I agree. Until Kassidy is found, I don't want to be alone."

Ax shifted his gaze. "Connor?"

"Already planned on it," Connor replied, clearly understanding Ax's unspoken question.

Ax stood, signaling to everyone the little meeting was over. "Report back if necessary. Otherwise, stick with her until you hear otherwise. I will have Neil, Matt, and Ryan, keep eyes on the house tonight." After giving his orders, he looked back at her. "When we have information we can share regarding your stepsister, I'll pass it along."

She tried to force a smile but couldn't do it. "Thank you. I appreciate it." She watched Ax leave the room and looked over at Connor. For the foreseeable future, he was her bodyguard. Becca almost shook her head. When he'd first told her what he did at the café, her first thought had been *I wouldn't complain about having you as a bodyguard.* And now he was exactly that. While she couldn't complain about the extra time they'd spend together, she sincerely wished it was for a very different reason.

Next to her, Connor stood and moved to speak with Keith. Both kept their voices low, making it impossible to catch anything they said. She heard the door behind her click and then Connor's hand came down on her shoulder.

"Don't worry. Nothing will happen to you—I won't let it."

FIFTEEN

ZANE YANKED the last shard of glass from his hand and wrapped a T-shirt around it. It had taken him years, but he'd learned to control his temper. At least most of the time. Tonight it had been either put a bullet through Espanto's skull or his fist through the glass cabinet door. Considering the blood soaking the T-shirt already, Zane wished he'd gone with the bullet to the asshole's head.

When it comes to tracking people, he's one of your best, he reminded himself again. It was the only reason the screwup was still breathing and not being weighted down and dumped in the Potomac River.

Grabbing the vodka, he twisted off the cap and took a long swig straight from the bottle. He'd given the guy specific, easy-to-follow instructions. Exactly what guys like Espanto needed. Not once since he'd come to work for him had Espanto ever not done exactly what he'd been ordered.

Until tonight.

Rather than follow orders, he'd tried using his brain and gone after Becca André. If he'd gotten her, Zane still would've ripped the asshole a new one for not following orders, but at least they'd finally have the bitch. He hadn't given Espanto a

chance to explain how she got away before knocking him uncon-
scious and having his sorry ass dragged from the room. One of
his best or not, there were consequences when you screwed up.
Espanto and everyone else in the organization knew it.

And it didn't matter to him how she managed it. What he
cared about was she'd slipped through Espanto's fingers, and no
doubt contacted the fucking cops.

Damn it. Zane slammed the bottle down. Everyone in his
organization played a specific role, and there was a reason he
used guys like Hammer and not Espanto for grabs. No matter
how many self-defense or karate classes a person had taken, they
weren't getting away from Hammer unless they shot him dead.
Espanto didn't have the same skill set. He was good at sticking
to the shadows and being unseen, so he could report back.

Before tonight, his prey might have been nervous, but now,
because of his boy's screwup, she knew someone was after her.
If she were smart, she'd never go anywhere alone again. She
might even look into hiring round-the-clock personal protection.
If he was Becca, he would, and she certainly had the resources to
do it. Either action would make getting his hands on her so he
could turn her over to Dale much more difficult.

He reached for the vodka and took another hit from the
bottle. At least the asshole had followed one of his orders, and
now Zane would be able to track most if not all of her
movements.

As soon as Becca left her house, Espanto called in and let
Zane know the house was empty. When he got the update, he'd
reached out to his contact at the alarm monitoring company and
had her turn off the system so one of his boys could go in.
Shawn had slipped inside the house and planted a few nearly-
impossible-to-find tracking devices on items she often took with
her. Shawn had done similar jobs for the organization before, so
he knew not to disturb anything else in the house. Even a book
out of place could alert an individual that someone had been in
a room.

While at it, Shawn also had just enough time to leave behind a few well-hidden listening devices in a couple areas of the house. He wouldn't be able to see Becca and anyone else who visited, but he'd hear a lot of what she said. Then, as Zane arranged, the system went back on after Shawn left the house, leaving Becca none the wiser.

Zane took a final drink of vodka and screwed the cap back on. The combination of time and alcohol had defused his anger enough, so he was no longer thinking about having a 9mm bullet put through Espanto's skull regardless of how useful he was.

Switching on the audio equipment Shawn left him, he sat with his feet up on the table and opened the app, which would track the GPS devices now hidden inside her belongings.

"Let's see if you're home."

SIXTEEN

HE THOUGHT she'd been tight-lipped during the ride from the hospital to Elite Force. But she'd been completely nonverbal the entire trip from the firm to her house. Connor didn't know what it meant.

Did she think Ax and everyone working the case had lost their minds in thinking Kassidy was some kind of criminal? Hell, this morning even he'd initially had his doubts that Kassidy was a suspect. The evidence gathered so far pointed in that exact direction, whether Becca wanted to accept it or not.

Had Becca agreed to hire protection because she feared the same people she believed forced Kassidy to steal research were now after her?

Or was she quiet because she was trying to come to terms with the truth that her stepsister wasn't who she thought she was? Something he knew from experience was never easy.

He hoped it was the last reason. The sooner she accepted Kassidy was most likely a suspect and not a victim, the better.

After following her into the kitchen, he dropped his two bags on the floor. One held the extra clothes he always kept in his SUV for unexpected assignments such as this. The other was his tactical go-bag. It contained everything from extra magazines for his gun to a full first aid kit. He hoped he didn't need anything inside the bag, but with so many unknowns, he needed to be prepared.

Before Becca even removed her sneakers, she reset the house alarm. "I need chocolate," she announced, tossing her wristlet and house key onto the table.

Some people drowned their problems in alcohol. If she wanted to drown them in candy, he wasn't going to stop her. Besides, filling up on chocolate was probably a lot better for her than a bottle or two of wine.

She searched through a cabinet and pulled out a fancy-looking gold box. "Want some?" Becca asked, holding the box out toward him. The name Favre was written across the cover in a font so elegant it was almost difficult to read.

If he'd experienced the day Becca had, he'd be going for a beer, not food. But he liked junk food, especially chocolate, as much as the next guy. "Sure."

He opened the box, hoping for a guide explaining what was in each candy. There was nothing worse than getting one filled with that weird orange crap they often covered with perfectly good chocolate, ruining it for the unsuspecting candy lover. No such guide was inside this box. He'd have to take his chances. Connor selected one and hoped the odd shape on top was an almond covered with chocolate, and not some other weird sugary creation.

"Is this a new company?" He'd let Becca get her candy fix before asking the tough questions.

Becca plucked a chocolate from the box. "You've never had Favre? You're in for a treat." She popped the candy into her mouth and reached for a second. "I'm taking this upstairs with us, but help yourself to anything you want."

The beer he knew she kept in the fridge sounded good, but he never drank when on an assignment. Instead, he took a few cans of flavored seltzer water out and followed her upstairs.

All her bedroom lights were already on when they entered

the room. "I left in a hurry." Leaving the Favre box on the night-stand, she removed a towel from the bed and walked into the bathroom. She came back out carrying a glass of wine.

"When Graham called, I'd just gotten in the hot tub to relax. A lot of good it did me." She set the almost-full glass down and raked both hands through her already-messy hair. "I keep hoping I'll wake up and find that this whole day has actually been one long nightmare."

He understood her sentiments, and if he had the power to change the events of the past twenty-four hours for her, he would.

"Your boss thinks Kassidy is a criminal." Becca went for the gold box again. She didn't even look inside. Instead, she pulled out a dark-colored square and raised it toward her lips. "Keith does too. I could tell. What about you? Neither of them knows Kassidy, but you do. Do you agree with them?"

It looked like he didn't need to ask the tough questions. She was jumping right into the conversation they needed to have. "It's not the answer you want but, yeah. I don't think Kassidy was forced to steal the research."

"You're right, it's not what I want to hear." Her eyelids drifted closed as her shoulders slumped. "But the more I think about everything said tonight, the more I agree."

He hated hearing the resignation in her voice, but accepting it now would make it easier when Kassidy was found and the truth became public knowledge.

Becca backed up and sat cross-legged on the bed. "A bunch of times over the summer I caught her lies. I told myself she was probably involved with a married man again." She rolled her eyes. "Kassidy has never been bothered by a man's marital status."

"What did she lie about?" She might think they weren't important, but who knew what tidbit of info might help them track down Kassidy.

"Silly things. Like one day, she said she arranged to visit

with my mom while up in New York. Less than twenty minutes later, I got a call from Mom, and she had no idea Kassidy was heading up that way. Another time she supposedly flew out to the Lafayette Laboratory branch in Austin, Texas. When she got back, the airport tags on her luggage were from Florida. Unless the states have moved around, Texas and Florida are not neighbors."

Becca's information didn't surprise him. It also didn't help him much.

"It probably wouldn't have changed the outcome, but I wish I'd confronted her."

He had no reason to believe Kassidy was violent. But, given the circumstances, it was possible she or maybe someone she was working with would've done whatever necessary to carry out their plan—even if it had meant harming Becca. "You're right. It wouldn't have changed anything."

"Do you think Mom and Robert have been contacted?"

"Yeah. The FBI would've sent someone from the New Haven office to visit them as soon as they got involved. Someone would've reached out to Kassidy's mom too."

She nodded and looked down at the box in her lap. After a quick assessment of its contents, she selected a treat, put the cover back on, and set the box on the nightstand. "Robert must be going nuts. Kassidy's his baby and, although he'd never admit it, she's always been his favorite."

Connor remembered Robert Buchanan. Under normal circumstances, he couldn't picture the man being anything but calm and cool without a hair out of place. Whenever a person's child was involved, regardless of the child's age, people acted and behaved in ways completely out of character.

"It's too late to call them tonight. First thing tomorrow, I'll do it," Becca said. "And speaking of tomorrow, what the heck am I going to tell everyone? It's not like people aren't going to notice you there."

No doubt whoever tried to grab her tonight knew where she

worked. Going anywhere near her office was a terrible idea. "You're not going to work." He didn't care if women hated being told what to do or not. Her safety came first.

Both her eyebrows rocketed toward her hairline. "Uh, yes, I am, Connor. Much like with your job, I can't call in sick whenever I feel like it. And while sometimes I can work from home, tomorrow it's not possible. I have meetings. Ones I cannot skip, and none can be rescheduled."

Even bringing her back here put him on edge. It'd seemed the best option for the night, though, since his teammates were watching the house. If anyone got past any of them, which was highly unlikely, and forced his way in, the security system would alert him immediately. In the morning, Connor intended to reassess the situation and move to a more secure location if necessary.

"Whoever is after you knows where you live. The jerk who attacked you tonight must have been watching the house and then followed you to the hospital. Trust me, he or whoever he's working for knows where you work too."

"Then I must have imagined you saying, and I quote, 'Don't worry. Nothing will happen to you—I won't let it.'"

At another time he would've laughed at her imitation of his voice. "Becca, you know you didn't." He mentally swore because he knew, regardless of what he said next, she would object. "I'd take a bullet to keep you safe."

"Elite Force must really pay you well." Becca muttered the comment softly, but he still heard it.

"Whether you took Ax's suggestion and hired the firm or not, I'd already planned to not leave you alone again until this is over. The firm and my paycheck have nothing to do with my willingness to do whatever it takes to keep you safe." And when he said "whatever," he meant it, even if it came down to taking someone else's life to stop them from harming her. "Going to work tomorrow is an unnecessary risk. I'm sure the senator would agree with me."

She stared at him, her lips slightly parted. What that meant he didn't know, and he figured it was better not to guess. Finally, she ran her tongue over her bottom lip and reached for his hand. "I'm glad you're here, and I'm not trying to make things more difficult for you. But it's important I attend my meetings. One took me months to arrange. Just let me go in tomorrow. While I'm with him, I'll explain the situation to Ted, and I won't go back until you tell me it's safe."

Arguing his point wouldn't get him anywhere, except perhaps kicked out. "One day, and you'll do exactly what I tell you. If I see anyone suspicious, we're out of there. Even if it means dragging you out against your will. Understand?"

A HEAVY ARM pinned her in place, making it possible to move. "We're going to take a little drive together, princesa*." The owner of the voice stood so close she felt the rise and fall of his chest as he breathed. "Don't make this hard and you won't get hurt," the unseen captor said.*

Despite the warning, she opened her mouth to scream. Not a sound came out. Frantic, she searched for help. Connor had promised to keep her safe. Why wasn't he there? She clawed at the arm holding her, but its owner seemed unaffected. Desperate to get away, she drove the heel of her favorite pumps down on his foot.

Becca's eyes flew open, and she searched the darkness. *It was a dream.*

It was Connor's arm across her stomach pinning her in place, not the creep from the parking garage. She was safe in her bed, and one of the best security systems money could buy was turned on. She had her own personal bodyguard asleep next to her. His 9mm Glock sat on the nightstand, loaded and ready if Connor needed to use it. She prayed he didn't, but she couldn't deny that knowing he had it nearby did make her feel better. And there were other employees from the firm outside her home, keeping watch.

Nothing is going to happen to me, she reminded herself.

Despite the words, her thoughts returned to the hospital. Maybe she should've tried to get a look at the creep's face. The police still might not have him in custody, but at least if she'd been able to give them a description, they'd have something to work with. At the time, getting away had been her only priority, and not once had she looked back to even check the distance separating them as she ran.

If the jerk had followed her from the house to the hospital, had he followed her to other places today? The man at lunch had definitely made her uncomfortable, but she dismissed him as a possibility. She hadn't heard any hint of an accent in her unwelcome bench companion's voice. But the guy who'd gone after her tonight definitely had one.

What about the man who thought pairing a suit with work boots was a good idea? It had looked as if he was headed in her direction as she walked to her car. Had he planned to grab her there, but then for some reason decided to wait?

She envisioned him crossing to the elevators. *Yeah, no way was he the guy who went after me earlier.* Mr. Suit and Work Boots had been huge. Only perhaps a miracle would've allowed her simple self-defense tactics to work on a man like him.

Lying in bed and running the whole event continuously through her head was getting her nowhere. Instead, she should close her eyes and try to get back sleep, because the alarm clock would go off at the same time it always did whether she'd gotten enough rest or not. Unfortunately, at the moment, she was more awake than if she'd downed three or four espressos in a row. Of course, when it was time to get out of bed, she'd probably be dead tired.

Becca ran her fingers gently across Connor's arm as she inched closer to him. If she couldn't sleep, then she'd at least lie there and ponder more pleasant thoughts.

Ever since their afternoon picnic, the feelings she'd had for him over fifteen years ago had started to resurface. Her short stay at his house had accelerated the process and, assuming he didn't suddenly disappear from her life again, he'd soon be planted in her heart.

Before tonight, she'd worried that was a disaster in the making. Now she didn't know what to expect. Every one of Connor's colleagues probably accepted that during certain assignments their lives would be at risk. However, tonight he'd gone out of his way to tell her his position with the firm had nothing to do with his willingness to protect her at any cost.

Starting with the day they met up in the café, he'd been honest and upfront with her. She had no reason to believe he was being anything but that tonight. And any individual, man or woman, willing to protect another no matter what wasn't hanging around just for the sex. Especially when he could easily get it from plenty of other women. His feelings toward her might not be approaching the big L-word like hers, but she didn't doubt he cared her. And for now, knowing she was important to him was enough.

"What's bothering you?" Connor said, his hand suddenly closing over her fingers.

"How did you know I was awake?" She hadn't made a sound and had barely moved since waking up. Could the man see in the dark?

He tucked her closer to him and kissed her cheek. "I'm a light sleeper. As soon as your fingers moved against my arm, I woke up." He linked their hands together.

His revelation didn't surprise her. "Sorry. I didn't mean to wake you."

"You were out cold, snoring away and drooling like a baby. What woke you?"

"I don't snore," she said.

Connor chuckled. "If you say so. But you didn't answer me."

"Nightmare, and now I'm wide awake."

He released her hand and slipped his fingers under her T-shirt. "Since we're both awake, we should enjoy ourselves." His hand closed over her breast as his lips came down on hers, banishing any thoughts of her hellish night or what awaited her tomorrow.

SEVENTEEN

KASSIDY, you're a selfish jerk. For the umpteenth time, Becca imagined slapping her stepsister and then tossing every foul word in the English language at her. Unfortunately, she couldn't do it. All she could do was mentally curse as she sent a final email to a colleague and powered off her computer.

Connor had been uneasy since they left her house. His mood hadn't improved as she dragged him from one meeting to another. It had hit an all-time low since they left her final one for the day and returned to her office. With all her obligations over, he wanted her out of the building and back to her place, where he had complete control over who came and went.

She'd never admit it, but she was anxious to get out of the building as well. Normally, having people around didn't bother her. Today she kept looking at each and every face, wondering if one of them was behind the kidnapping attempt the night before, regardless of whether it was a person she knew or not. At this point, except for Connor and perhaps the senator, she didn't know who else in the building to trust.

Becca checked her briefcase one last time. She had no idea when she'd set foot in her office again. If she hoped to get work accomplished from home, she needed to take everything today, because Connor would never let her come back.

The knock on the office door brought Connor to his feet, and his hand went for the pistol under his jacket. "I'll answer it."

I don't think bad guys knock on doors she wanted to tell him, but kept silent. Connor protected people for a living. He knew what he was doing, and she'd let him do his job.

"Good, you're still here," Senator Lynch said, entering the room.

She'd explained the situation to him the first chance she got. He'd been speechless, a condition Ted Lynch never experienced. She might love him much like an uncle, but the man loved to hear his own voice. Regardless of the topic, he never found himself without a comment or opinion. Until today.

Becca closed the briefcase and slipped the strap onto her shoulder. "I'm getting ready to leave. Did you need anything before I go?"

Connor would have a fit, but if the senator needed something, she couldn't tell him no. Family friend or not, he was her boss and he expected her to do her job.

Senator Lynch closed the door. "No, I'm all set. I wanted to ask you again to come and stay with us. Kathleen and I would feel much better if you did."

He'd made the same offer earlier. Since she had a second shadow named Connor Anderson, she didn't see how she'd be any safer at Ted's house than at her own. And Connor really had been her shadow today. The only time she'd been alone was when she used the private bathroom attached to her office.

As a general rule, she treated Ted the same as she would any other senator while in the office. This afternoon, the only other person in the room with them was Connor. He already knew Ted Lynch was a close family friend. Becca came around her desk and hugged the man she'd grown up calling Uncle Ted. "I appreciate it, but I'll be fine." She forced a smile for Ted's sake. "Connor will make sure I'm back to work soon."

Hopefully. She had full confidence in Connor's ability to keep her safe; it was whether the situation would be straightened out quickly that she doubted.

The senator's frown remained. "If you change your mind, our doors are open to you. No need to call first. Just come." He hugged her back, nearly breaking all her ribs in the process. "Please keep me updated on everything. Including any news regarding Kassidy."

Becca caught Connor shake his head slightly and then point toward the door. "We need to go. I'll call you when I can," she promised.

Many of the office doors remained closed when they stepped out into the hallway, making it difficult to gauge how many still slaved away. "Stay on my left," he instructed as she closed and locked the office door.

He'd told her to do the same earlier. It hadn't required much thought to figure out why he wanted her there. Connor was right-handed. If he needed to draw and fire his weapon, he didn't want her in the way.

CONNOR MOVED, positioning his body between the elevator door and Becca. As the doors opened, his hand moved toward his weapon. He hadn't seen anyone suspicious so far today, but if someone was waiting on the other side, he wanted to be ready. He did a quick sweep of the area. "Let's go." He didn't need to tell her to hurry. She kept up with him despite the three-inch heels she wore.

He got her locked inside the SUV before sweeping the area again and walking around to the driver side. Whoever was after Becca wouldn't just give up, and parking garages like this were great spots to grab someone.

"Do you think I should've accepted Ted's offer to stay with him and Kathleen?" she asked when he got behind the wheel.

"No. There's nothing to say someone wouldn't go after you

there." He ignored the posted speed limit and drove down the ramp toward the exit. "You'd be putting the senator and his wife in danger."

"You're right. I didn't consider that." She pulled out the long chopstick-looking decorations holding her hair up in a tight bun and dropped them into her purse. If they got into a tight bind, he could probably use the ridiculous things as weapons.

They remained silent as they left the parking garage behind and joined the usual busy D.C. traffic.

She didn't speak again until they turned onto Independence Avenue. "Any word from Ax?"

The car in front of them just made it through before the traffic light changed, forcing Connor to stop. "Nothing." He glanced into the rearview mirror, taking note of each vehicle behind them. "I got a message from Ryan. All clear at your house." There wasn't anything more boring than surveillance. Sometimes it was the only way to get information. Or, in this case, make sure a location remained safe so they could return to it at least temporarily. "When we get to your place, pack enough for a week."

Taking her back home last night had been a calculated risk. Last night the kidnapper had failed, and in his experience, when a plan went south, you needed to regroup. So, after discussing it with Ax, they'd decided with three team members outside and him inside it'd be safe for Becca to sleep in her own bed.

Tonight they'd stay somewhere else, allowing Ryan, Neil, and Matt to get back to searching for Kassidy and whoever was after Becca.

"If it's been quiet at my house, why can't we stay there again?"

The light turned green, and he crossed the intersection. "The asshole would've kept a low profile last night after you got away. With Neil, Matt, and Ryan outside all night and me inside, it was safe. But from now on we'll avoid any places you normally visit."

Turning the corner, he watched in the mirror as the vehicle directly behind him continued straight. However, the white one two cars back with heavily tinted windows followed them.

"Where are we staying?"

They drove through another intersection, and he sped up. The driver of the white car behind him almost took out a dude on a motorcycle who managed to sneak his way into the traffic.

"Somewhere safe." Connor gripped the steering wheel, half his attention on the white car behind them and the other on the traffic. He knew this area well. The next right- hand turn was a one-way, so it wasn't an option. Thanks to the red light up ahead, taking a left was out too. A line of traffic six cars long waited for the light to change.

Without using his turn signal, he went down the next possible street, cutting off another vehicle in the process. As expected, the driver of the BMW he cut off laid on the horn and threw him the bird. "Check and see if there's a white car behind us."

Becca turned in her seat. "One with dark windows?"

Damn it. "Yeah." He never should've taken her into the office. He should've let her rest for a few hours last night and then made her pack her bags.

Up ahead the traffic light switched from yellow to red and Connor accelerated, making it through the intersection without getting hit by any other vehicles. He checked the mirror again. The white car had run the light too, but as he watched, another vehicle cut between them.

"Keep an eye on it. And see if you can get a look at the license plate." He took the first on-ramp to the highway he reached.

While the jerk could be leaving D.C. like half the cars on the road, his instincts told him otherwise. So before he could get her anywhere safe, he had to get rid of the tail behind him. His best bet was getting her back to Elite Force. Once inside, no one would be able to get close to her. He ran various routes through his head.

"He's still there, but now there are two cars between us," she said.

Tearing his eyes away from the road, he checked the mirror. An old lady barely able to see over the steering wheel was driving the car directly behind them. He couldn't see the driver of the second car between them and their tail.

"Watch out!" Becca shouted.

Connor hit the brake in time to avoid crashing into the large SUV that had suddenly pulled in front of him and then immediately slowed down.

Shit. Was this guy working with the dude in the white sedan, or was the driver of the SUV just an asshole? Trapping a vehicle and forcing it to stop wasn't uncommon, but doing it on a busy highway with plenty of witnesses around was risky.

Traffic around them remained heavy, making it impossible to even try to cut into another lane as they crossed into Virginia. Despite the driver's previous recklessness to cut them off, the SUV in front of them never went over the speed limit.

A car in the next lane sped up and then exited the highway, leaving an opening. Connor jerked the wheel, taking its spot, then accelerated past the SUV he'd previously been stuck behind. If the two vehicles were working together, he'd rather have them both behind him.

Connor spotted the next exit off the highway. "Hold on."

He pressed the accelerator to the floor and waited until the last possible moment to take the exit. Despite the "dangerous curve" warning, he didn't slow down. He ignored the stop sign and merged onto the road, flying past the other vehicles as if they stood still.

"Anything behind us?" he asked.

Becca twisted in her seat and looked out the back window. "I don't see anyone."

He wasn't taking any chances. Connor passed a busy shopping center and through two more sets of traffic lights before he hopped back on the highway.

SHE THOUGHT she'd ridden some jaw-dropping roller coasters over the years. However, compared to the little drive she'd just experienced with Connor, even the most thrilling roller coaster in the world seemed tame. How they'd managed to avoid getting into an accident was beyond her. More than once she'd squeezed her eyes shut and prayed, fully expecting to hear the sound of tires squealing followed by the crunching of metal.

Instead, all she'd heard was the blood thundering in her ears. Actually, she could still hear it even though they were safely behind the security gates of Elite Force and on their way up to the fourth floor.

Afraid of distracting him, she'd kept her mouth shut since Connor hopped back on the highway. Before they had an audience, she needed to take responsibility for what they'd just gone through. "I'm sorry."

"For?"

"Not listening to you. By going into work, I put you in danger." The elevator reached the fourth floor and the doors slid open.

He pressed the button, closing the doors and giving them some privacy. "You put yourself in danger."

They were both right. Her refusal to listen had put them both in danger. And if anything had happened to him because of her stupid decision, she never would've forgiven herself.

He moved in closer and touched her face. "It's done and you're safe. But from now on we'll do things my way."

She'd learned her lesson. At least until the danger passed, he wouldn't get a single argument from her. "Got it. I promise."

The door to the team's meeting room she'd sat in last night was closed. Leaving her, Connor entered, shutting it behind him.

Obviously, whatever was being discussed by heaven knew who on the other side wasn't meant for her ears. Perhaps for the moment, it was for the best anyway. She was already feeling a bit like Alice after her little trip down the rabbit hole. Who knew how she'd feel if she heard the conversation taking place?

When Connor came back out, he wasn't alone. "Give Mad Dog your clothing size." Putting an arm over her shoulder, he gestured toward the woman who followed him out of the meeting room. "She'll take care of it, and we'll wait here until she gets back."

She never would've guessed this was Mad Dog. Becca could easily picture the woman starring in movies rather than working for a security firm. "Uh, sure."

Becca couldn't remember the last time someone had picked out her clothes. She didn't see a way around it. Even if Connor agreed to take her shopping, which he never would, she had no desire to risk going anywhere near a store. And after their high-speed race to the firm, she knew going back to her house for clothes was out of the question.

Connor's coworker handed her a notepad and pen. "Men." She shook her head and extended her hand. "My normal friends call me Maddie." She pointed in Connor's direction. "He's not what I call normal."

Despite the gravity of the situation, she couldn't contain her smile. "Becca. Connor's mentioned you. It's nice to finally put a face to the name."

"Please make a list of any essentials you need. Shampoo, toothpaste, whatever," Maddie said. "And if you prefer a specific brand of anything put it down. I'll do my best to get it. Somewhere on there write down your clothing and shoe size."

She started her list, keeping it as a simple as possible. All things considered, what brand of toothpaste she used seemed unimportant for the foreseeable future.

"This should be good." She handed the notepad back, glad it was Maddie, AKA Mad Dog, and not one of Connor's male colleagues doing the shopping. Since she had no idea how long it'd be before she returned home, she'd added tampons, razors, and shaving cream to the list. Becca couldn't picture someone like Keith carrying a box of tampons and women's razors to a store checkout.

Maddie read over the list and glanced back at her. "I won't be long. Are you sure you didn't forget anything?" Her eyes darted in Connor's direction before meeting Becca's again, her real question clear. The other woman wanted to know if Becca wanted condoms in addition to mint toothpaste and shampoo. As much as she enjoyed sex with Connor, it and condoms were the furthest things from her mind right now.

Clearly Connor understood what his coworker was refer-ring to as well. "If we need anything not on the list, I've got it."

"Whatever you say. See you both soon."

She watched the other woman walk away. "She's not what I expected." She could avoid her real questions and pretend this was any other normal day. But talking about his coworkers or the weather wouldn't get her answers. "What's next?"

"When Mad Dog gets back, we'll head to one of the firm's safe houses."

There he went again, using a word she'd never thought she'd associate with her life.

"You'll need to leave your cell phone here."

Go without her cell phone? What if someone in her family needed her? Or the senator? "Why? I don't see how having my phone with me will help whoever went after me."

He led her into a small kitchen and went to the commercial-grade coffee maker on one counter. "Until we know who's after you and perhaps Kassidy, we don't know what capabilities they have. With the right equipment, any cell phone can be easily tracked."

"I guess I won't be checking my email while we're away either."

Connor handed her a paper cup before he took a sip from his own. "Where we're headed, there isn't any internet."

The last time she'd gone with no internet for more than a few hours, she'd been away at summer camp. It had been perhaps the single worst experience of her life until this week. And, truthfully, she wasn't sure she'd survive without access to the internet and her email. "Tell me we'll at least have running water."

If he said they'd be drinking bottled water and using an outhouse, she'd ask if she could sleep here on the floor instead.

"Water yes, but if you want electricity, it'll cost you." He winked at her, but his attempt at humor did nothing to improve her mood.

"THANK YOU." Becca accepted the bags from Maddie and placed them near her purse and briefcase. She didn't bother to ask how much she owed her. No doubt whatever the woman had spent on clothes and toiletries would be added to her final bill from the firm—assuming she lived long enough to get a final bill.

"Not a problem." Maddie poured herself a cup of what masqueraded as coffee.

During her life, she'd had a lot of coffee, but what Connor had poured for her earlier was the most bitter she'd ever tasted. She'd poured half of it out so she could add a ridiculous amount of milk and sugar to it. Somehow he'd managed to get down not one, but two cups of the stuff black.

Becca watched Connor's coworker add several sugar packets to the cup before taking a sip of the black liquid.

"It wasn't on the list, but I picked up a few magazines and a couple books. If you want to take it, I have a book of Sudoku puzzles in my car."

"I'm more of a crossword person, but thanks."

"Anytime," she said before leaning against the counter. "You'll be fine. Connor's one of the best here."

"She meant to say the best." Connor's voice came from the doorway behind her.

He'd left to discuss final arrangements with Ax more than thirty minutes ago. At least that's what he'd told her. It wouldn't surprise her if they'd been discussing other things as well. Things they couldn't or wouldn't say in her presence.

Maddie rolled her eyes. "I don't know how you fit your damn head through the door, Anderson." She took another sip of the world's worst coffee and pushed off the counter. "Good luck, Becca. You have my sympathies being stuck with him." She walked out before Becca could come up with a response that didn't make her sound like she'd lost her mind. Because, as much as she hated the need to hide away in a safe house, she didn't mind for a moment having Connor to herself.

Connor moved inside the room. He had a large backpack slung over one shoulder and two other large bags in his hand. "Ready?" he asked.

She hadn't seen the white car again after they exited the highway. And nothing Connor said during the final stretch of the mad dash back to the firm suggested he believed they were still being followed. But what if they had been?

What if someone was sitting outside now, waiting for them to exit the parking lot? Or what if the people after her did have the technology necessary to locate her cell phone, and they'd tracked it back to the firm?

"Do you think anyone's out there, waiting for us to leave?"

"It's possible." He sounded unconcerned as he readjusted the strap over his shoulder. "But they won't see us."

"Let me guess—the firm has developed some kind of technology that makes cars invisible, right?"

"It'd make my job a hell of a lot easier." He took her hand and gave it a squeeze. "Trust me, you'll see. If someone is out there watching the main exits, they won't see us."

She followed him down the hall, past the elevator they'd used to come upstairs, and to another one at the far end of the building. Inside he pressed the button marked with a large letter G. "Are we off to a secret cave?"

He only chuckled as the door opened, revealing a well-lit enclosed parking area. "Only the firm's bigwigs are allowed to park down here, so they don't get their hair wet when it rains. All company-owned vehicles are stored down here too. We're using one of those. Ryan will leave in my SUV and drive around for a while in case anyone's out there watching for it. Later he'll bring it back here."

Connor led her past a nice display of imported vehicles, each parked in a spot labeled with a lofty title indicating just who each car belonged to, and letting her know how well the firm's management must be paid.

The taillights of a midnight-blue two-door with windows so dark no one would ever see who was on the other side flashed. After popping the trunk, he dropped two of his bags inside and then added hers before slamming it. She couldn't help but notice the bag he kept with him was the same one he'd referred to as a tactical go-bag when she'd asked him about it last night. She hadn't asked for a full inventory. Still, she knew whatever items he kept in the bag were ones she'd never thought would be part of her daily life.

He put the last bag in the back, within arm's reach, and started the car.

She didn't bother to ask where they were headed. One, it didn't matter, and two, she doubted he'd tell her anyway.

She remained quiet as he drove through the garage, down a narrow two-way tunnel to a security gate. He punched in a code and the gates moved aside, allowing them to exit onto a street behind the firm. At the moment, except for them, there wasn't a soul around. Maybe they would make it out of the city without being detected.

"We've got a possible location on Kassidy," Connor shared, breaking the silence.

She suspected neither the FBI nor any one of the other government agencies involved had obtained the location. Going through the proper channels to get information from companies, regardless of the type, took time. Even considering the urgency of the situation, enough time hadn't passed since she told Connor about the text messages and call from Kassidy. If Kassidy's location was known, a tech-savvy individual, most likely one from the firm's cyber division, had hacked into whatever company controlled the apps her stepsister used.

"Where is she?"

"Sorry, I can't share anything else."

Was he joking? "Seriously, Connor, where does the firm think she is?"

"If I could tell you, I would. Right now all I'm allowed to share is that we have a possible location and that HRT, along with agents from the FBI and Air Force OSI, are looking into it."

He's only the messenger. Her mental reminder didn't alleviate her annoyance. "Who the hell am I going to tell? I'm going to be stuck in some stupid safe house, probably in the middle of nowhere. Is your boss afraid I'll tell a chipmunk or maybe a bunny rabbit?" Crossing her arms, she glared out the window. "When they find her, will they let me know?" Would they keep her in the dark about that too?

Connor took the Interstate 495 West exit and merged with traffic. Unlike the last time they'd been in a car together, Becca didn't feel the need to close her eyes and pray.

"Ax will contact me when they have Kassidy."

EIGHTEEN

A HORRIBLE CRAMP in her neck forced Becca to open her eyes, and she adjusted her position in the seat. Since falling asleep, a light rain had started up, but the dark clouds off in the distance threatened a more powerful storm later tonight. Rubbing her neck, she studied the view. The last she remembered, they'd been on the highway heading west. They were no longer on a highway, and she didn't recognize anything around them.

"Have a nice nap?" Connor asked.

Except for the cramp in her neck, she couldn't complain because this had been the first sleep she'd had in days where a faceless person hadn't grabbed her. "Not bad. Where are we?" Regardless of their current location, she hoped they were almost to their destination because she was in desperate need of a bathroom break. "And will we be stopping soon?"

"We just crossed into Chester Gap."

They could be halfway to Florida for all she knew. She'd never heard of any town or city by that name. "I'm guessing we're still somewhere in Virginia."

He nodded and turned up the speed of the windshield wipers as the drizzle turned into a sudden downpour. "Not far from Shenandoah National Park."

She still wouldn't be able to pinpoint exactly where they were on a map, but she did know they were far west of D.C. and Alexandria. Since she wouldn't need to get them home when this was over, his answer was sufficient.

"We'll be at the cabin in less than five minutes."

Cabin. The word brought up images of her one and only trip to summer camp. As a counselor in training, she'd shared a tiny log cabin with a wood plank floor and rustic bunks with four other girls. *He promised running water.*

When he turned down a dirt road, she began to wonder if perhaps he'd lied about having water and electricity. A modest two-story structure that slightly resembled the cabins featured in every historical movie depicting rural frontier life in the nine-teenth century came into view. The only major differences between those homes and this one were the wires leading into the house and the swing hanging inside the screened-in porch on the left side of the building.

"When you said cabin, you really meant cabin." *Please let the inside be more up to date.*

"You won't have internet or cable, but you'll have everything else you do at home. More importantly, you'll be safe."

Becca accepted she'd be safe out here, especially with Connor. As for the rest, she'd reserve judgment until they got inside.

HE'D LIED. The cabin didn't have everything Becca had at home. She had an excellent central air-conditioning system, something he wished like hell the cabin had tonight. He'd changed into a sleeveless T-shirt, but even with the lousy A/C system installed in the home on, and all the ceiling fans going, he was dying. If they'd been anywhere else, he would've changed into a pair of light running shorts instead of his jeans. Unfortunately, running shorts would make keeping his Glock on his waist impossible. But Connor would gladly suffer a few nights of discomfort if it meant keeping Becca safe. Except for inside the firm, he couldn't think of anyplace safer than this.

On the television, the movie's hero drove down a one-way street in the wrong direction before catching up to the villain again and chasing him through the crowded city streets of Paris. Since he'd seen the movie, he already knew how it ended. Rather than keeping his attention focused on the screen, he kept it on Becca.

She'd changed too. Instead of wearing the expensive tailored suit from earlier, she had on a slightly too-tight tank top, not that he was complaining, and jean shorts. Later he planned to get her out of both. First, he'd give her a chance to decompress. She'd had a hell of a week, the kind that would've sent most women—hell, most men—into a crying fit.

No doubt about it, she'd experienced fear and worry. But she had a backbone. Despite the crap going on around her, she'd kept her head. He didn't know any other woman except Mad Dog who could've handled the week the way Becca had. And that only strengthened his desire to be with her.

In high school, she'd been more to him than just another girl to screw. She was that again and then some. He hadn't rekindled their acquaintance expecting much more than a few months of fun. Somehow, in the short time they'd been together, she'd worked her way into his affections. Where they'd ultimately end up, he had no damn clue, but for the first time in his adult life, he wanted to find out if she was the one.

"Something wrong? You're not watching the movie," Becca said, catching him looking at her instead of the television. "If you don't like it, we can put on a different one."

The cabin had no cable, but it did have a huge collection of movies. None of them held any interest for him. "Just thinking." He realized his colossal mistake after he spoke the words.

Becca muted the volume, confirming he should've given a different answer or kept his mouth shut. "About?"

He could lie. Tell her he was running security measures

through his head or thinking about what they should have for dinner. The fridge in the kitchen contained only cans of soda and bottled water, but the cabinets were filled with foods that had long shelf lives, such as pasta and tuna fish. If they didn't want to cook, the pantry closet held enough MREs to keep them fed for weeks.

But Connor hadn't lied to her once and starting now wasn't part of his plan.

"You."

"Do I want to know exactly what about me you're thinking about?" she asked with a combination of worry and suspicion.

Before her imagination took off and she concocted what she thought was on his mind, he pulled her onto his lap. "You've impressed the hell out of me the past few days. If my sister was going through the shit you are, she'd be a crying disaster. I haven't seen you lose it once."

Becca slid her fingers over his shoulder and up his neck before tracing the outermost part of his ear. "Breaking down wouldn't do me any good right now. I'll save it for after." She moved her hand and her fingers slipped down his neck instead. "Having you around has helped keep me from going crazy too."

"I'm not going anywhere."

She looked away, but her expression before she did told him enough. She had something on her mind but didn't want to ask the question. Usually a person did that because they were afraid they weren't going to like the answer.

"Your boss wouldn't like it if you did. He'd have to send Ryan out here," she offered in lieu of a question. But it didn't matter. Her statement filled him in on her true thoughts. He thought he'd cleared up her doubts about this thing between them. Either he'd failed, or the stress from the day was silently screwing with all her emotions.

"Ryan wouldn't complain, but I'd have to kill him if he did anything besides sit around and guard you," Connor answered.

"I don't let anyone, not even a close friend, mess with anything important to me."

"I'm not sure if I should be flattered by that statement or not."

"Bad choice of words. But you get the idea, right?"

She moved her face closer to his ear. "I think so, but maybe we can go upstairs and you can demonstrate. I'm more of a hands-on learner."

CONNOR STARED up at the ceiling. Moonlight from outside provided enough illumination for him to see the blades of the ceiling fan spinning and providing them with some additional relief from the heat because, even with the air conditioning cranked up, the temperature hovered around seventy-five degrees. Next to him, Becca slept—at least he assumed she slept—with her head his shoulder and one hand on his naked torso. The heat seeping from her body to his was only adding to his physical discomfort and making him sweat more. But he couldn't move away. He enjoyed having her close too much. However, he did wish she were this close while they slept in a room with well-functioning air-conditioning.

He kicked off the sheet covering his feet and focused on the raindrops pelting the windows and skylight, the sound almost hypnotic in the otherwise silent room.

The hand on his stomach slipped away as Becca turned onto her other side, and he heard her mutter Kassidy's name. He'd learned the first night she slept at his house that Becca often talked in her sleep. Sometimes he couldn't make out the words, but other times it was as clear as if she'd been wide awake.

Since Kassidy's activities were the reason Becca was in hiding, he wasn't surprised she was dreaming about the bitch tonight.

Damn, he hoped the team found her and dragged her ass

back to Virginia. The geniuses in cyber had hacked the app she'd used to call Becca, once again proving they could do things few people could. There was no guarantee she'd be there, soaking up the Caribbean sunshine, but it was a lead. And by now, Spike and the other team members assigned to finding her were on Saint Croix. Once they got Kassidy back, she'd be able to tell them who was after Becca so they could take them out of play too.

Part of him wished he was on the team going in. Considering what Becca had been through, he couldn't think of anything he'd enjoy more than seeing Kassidy carted back to Virginia in hand-cuffs. Asking to go along on the mission hadn't been an option, though. Becca needed him, and while he trusted everyone he worked with, it'd be a cold day in hell before he left her safety to anyone else.

Connor sat up. With Becca no longer using him as a pillow, he could make a trip downstairs for water. Becca rolled over in bed again and sat up before his feet touched the floor.

"Is something wrong?" He glanced back over, expecting her to tell him she'd had another nightmare.

Brushing the hair off her forehead, she crossed her legs in front of her. "Just can't sleep. I'm going to go downstairs and get a snack. Do want you anything?"

"I'll come with you. I'm a little hungry too." They might be in a secure location, but he'd rather she not leave his field of vision unless absolutely necessary. Standing, he grabbed his jeans from the floor and pulled them on. Usually at night, he removed his gun and the extra magazines from his belt. Tonight he'd intentionally left them in place; while the likelihood he'd need a weapon while they got a snack was almost nonexistent, he wasn't taking any chances.

The skylights in the hall provided enough illumination for them to walk downstairs without turning on any lights. When they reached the living room, they switched on the overhead ceiling fan and light before entering the kitchen and doing the same in there.

Becca went straight for the kitchen closet while he grabbed two bottles of water. "Anything specific you feel like?"

After handing one to Becca, he twisted off the cap on his and chugged down half the bottle. "What are our options?"

"Lots of microwave popcorn. Mixed nuts, a couple types of cookies, and some cheese-flavored crackers."

Sounded a bit like what he kept in his kitchen at home. "You pick. I don't care as long as it's edible."

Finished with the first bottle, he got a second one from the fridge. Before opening it, he pressed the cool plastic against the back of his neck. "When we get back, I need to tell Ax the A/C in this place needs to be fixed. Last time I was here it worked fine."

She put the mixed nuts on the table before carrying the popcorn to the microwave. "It could be worse. We could be stuck in here with no heat while the temps outside dipped below zero." Becca tossed the bag into the microwave and hit Start. "I don't know about you, but I'd rather be uncomfortably warm than freezing cold."

On this he disagreed. If they were cold, there was something he could do about it. The cabin had a huge fireplace in the living room and cords of wood stacked outside.

Over the sound of kernels popping, the rattle of rain hitting the windows increased, a clear indication the storm outside had intensified. A moment later, a flash of lightning streaked through the sky, followed soon after by a clap of thunder. Becca jumped, causing some of the nuts in the container she held to spill onto the table.

"Don't say it. I know it was only thunder. It just took me by surprise."

"Wasn't going to say a thing." He snagged a few of the nuts from the table. "I wasn't expecting it to storm like this tonight, either."

When the microwave dinged, they carried their late-night snack into the living room and switched on the television.

He flipped through the collection of DVDs, since, with no cable or internet in the house, if they wanted to watch anything, it had to be a movie. "It can storm all night, but I hope the power doesn't go out." It was uncomfortable enough in here with the little bit of cool air the system was pumping out and the fan going. If the power went out, it'd turn into a complete sauna.

Becca nudged him and laughed. "Afraid of the dark, tough guy?"

Connor parted his lips, prepared to answer.

Boom. The sound echoed through the room. He didn't need to hear it again to know it wasn't thunder.

Coming to his feet, he grabbed his gun and pulled Becca up.

Their car wasn't far from the front door, but he had no idea what might be waiting for them outside if they left the house. The bedroom was the best option, especially since he had no idea how many were coming in. While they might not be able to escape from the room, he'd have an unobstructed view of anyone who came down the hallway and tried to enter.

"Upstairs. Now." He ran, half-pulling Becca behind him.

The punk crossed into the living room as they reached the stairs. Lining up the gun's sights on the dude's chest, Connor pulled the trigger. The jerk dropped to the floor.

When they reached the top of the stairs, he pushed Becca in front of him. "Run!" he shouted, even though he knew it wasn't necessary.

Behind them the steps creaked, the sound confirming the punk on the floor downstairs had at least one friend with him.

Shit.

Slamming the door closed, he turned the lock. It wouldn't stop anyone, but it would buy him a few more seconds. In situations like this, every second counted.

Connor tossed her his cell phone. "Call 911." He trained his gun on the door. "Get in the closet and sit on the floor." While the closet's wooden door wouldn't stop a stray bullet, if she were inside, the asshole coming up the stairs wouldn't see her the second he entered the room, making it impossible for him to fire at her.

Fear rolled off her in waves, and it killed him that he couldn't comfort her.

She didn't hesitate to dash into the closet.

Please stay there. He didn't think she'd come out, but when people got scared, they didn't always act rationally.

Shotgun fire ripped through the silence moments before the bedroom door swung open.

A figure filled the entranceway as a clap of thunder momentarily filled the room. Connor aimed at the asshole's chest and squeezed the trigger.

The jerk staggered back before slumping to the floor.

He strained to hear anything else over the ringing in his ears. Did he have anyone else to worry about?

Only silence greeted him. While he preferred it to gunfire directed at him, he'd love to hear the sound of police sirens.

He started moving closer to the door and the prone figure on the floor. Blood pooled under the jerk. If he wasn't dead, he soon would be. Connor didn't know about the one downstairs. And he wasn't going down to find out.

Heavy footsteps came down the hall. Whoever was coming had heard the shots, so either he figured his buddy with the shotgun had done the shooting, or he had a death wish. Either way, he wouldn't be walking out of the house tonight.

As soon as he had a visual, Connor aimed at the newest player and fired.

Nothing happened.

Shit.

A shot rang out before he could clear the misfire or grab his backup weapon, grazing his arm before embedding itself in the wall.

Immediately another bullet ripped through the room, piercing one of the windows.

Dropping to a knee, Connor grabbed the spare gun from the bag near his feet. He fired off two rounds in rapid succession.

The flash from a bolt of lightning streaked through the room, allowing him to watch the body hit the floor.

GOD, she was never going to hear right again. Rubbing her ears, she tried to squeeze herself further into the corner of the small closet. She didn't know how many gunshots she'd heard since she'd been sitting in here. But she knew it'd been multiple ones, and at the moment, she had no idea if any of those bullets had found their way into Connor.

I wouldn't be alone in here if they'd killed him, she reminded herself. If whoever forced their way inside had killed Connor, they would've dragged her out of the house.

Unless they just haven't managed to find me yet.

Definitely not the kind of thought she should be having, yet Becca couldn't deny it was a possibility. At this very moment, they might be searching every room and the basement, looking for her. If that was the case, they'd find her eventually.

And then what? If Connor was dead, there would be no one to help her, and basic self-defense wouldn't do any good against a gun.

Please let him be okay. If anything had happened to him, she'd never forgive herself.

It took a moment for her to recognize the sound as a knock. A moment later, she heard Connor's voice.

"Becca. It's me."

Tears streaked down her cheeks, and she brushed them away with a hand.

"The police are here, and I'm opening the door."

When the door opened, she rushed forward and threw her arms around him.

"The threat's—"

Covering his lips with hers, she cut off whatever else he planned to say. At the moment, she didn't care about the words. He could tell her anything he wanted later.

She only cared that he was safe and there with her.

———

BECCA SQUEEZED HER EYES SHUT. The vision of the blood-soaked floor and the two bodies remained as she struggled to keep from puking again. She'd never been bothered by the sight of blood until tonight. Connor had suggested she keep her eyes closed when they left the room. She hadn't listened. And when he led her out of the bedroom and past the two intruders he'd shot upstairs, she'd thrown up all over the floor, mere inches from the intruder she recognized as the man from the parking garage who thought pairing work boots with a suit was a good idea.

Learning from her mistake, she took his advice when they passed the intruder he'd shot downstairs, who was also being worked on by paramedics.

Safely away from the gory sights, she had no desire to throw up again, especially with several of Connor's coworkers and the police on the porch with them. Taking several deep breaths, she tuned out the conversation they were having.

He's okay. Despite her reminder, she opened her eyes and looked over at Connor.

When she'd heard the first gunshot, she'd almost bolted for the door, intent on helping the man she was falling in love with. She'd even reached for the doorknob. Thankfully, cold reality hit her before she could exit the closet. She had no training whatsoever and no weapon. If she stepped out of the closet, she'd be more of a liability than anything else.

So, even though it had killed her to not know Connor's

condition, she'd stayed hidden in the closet as he'd instructed, until he came for her.

The uniformed police officer went back inside the house, leaving her and the other members of HRT on the porch alone. Surrounded by several highly trained armed individuals, she should feel safe, yet she didn't. Despite all the steps they'd taken, someone had still managed to find her, and she wanted to know how.

"How did they find us?"

Her question brought the conversation to a halt, and all eyes turned her way.

"We're not sure yet," Ax admitted. He crossed the porch and sat next to her on the swing. "Connor told you to leave your cell phone behind. Did you bring it along anyway?"

Becca shook her head, a little miffed that he immediately thought she'd done something wrong. "I left it and my laptop at the firm. I only brought the stuff Maddie picked up at the store, my purse, and briefcase."

Whatever silent message Ax sent Connor, he understood because he headed inside the house.

"At any point in the past few days, have either been where someone could get to them?" Ax asked.

"I almost always have my purse with me, and if I'm not at work, my briefcase is at home."

"Almost always?" he commented. "When was the last time you went out and didn't have it?"

Connor came back out and put her belongings on the small table. He didn't ask permission before dumping out the contents of her purse. As she watched him sort through the various items, she considered Ax's question. Across from Connor, Maddie started taking everything from the briefcase.

"I'm not sure. Maybe the night I went to get Graham at the hospital."

"You didn't have it with you when I picked you up," Connor

replied while he dug through the inside compartment of the purse.

He could dig all he wanted—the only things he'd find in the pockets were gum and maybe a few hair elastics. "But it would've been at home."

"Someone got to it." Connor held up an object that was most certainly not a pack of gum.

"Found another one." Maddie held out a similar-looking device.

Ax joined Connor and Maddie, leaving her to wonder how the items had ended up in her belongings. Even if she had left them at home and gone out, she always set the alarm. If anyone tried to get in, it would've gone off and the monitoring company would've alerted both her and the police. She hadn't received any calls from them since having the system installed.

"They got into my house again, didn't they?" As unlikely as it seemed, there was no other explanation. She left the swing so she could be part of the conversation and because she needed to be close to Connor.

Wrapping an arm around her, he pulled her against his side. Unfortunately, the physical contact didn't have the effect she'd hoped for.

"Looks like it. But we can get a location on them now." Connor held out the device he'd removed from her purse and dropped it into her hand. "We've used these. Unlike some tracking devices, these use the cell towers. They work similar to the way the locating device on a phone works. Since we have them, cyber will be able to find the son of a bitch who's after you."

NINETEEN

HE'D NEVER COMMITTED an act of violence. He preferred to leave that to others. It was better that lowlifes like Zane got their hands dirty than him.

This time Dale would make an exception. And he couldn't wait.

He'd start with Becca André.

While he'd known from the start she'd die, it hadn't been because he held any ill will toward her. No, her death simply would've been a necessary one after he got Kassidy's location from her. He'd been content to let Zane or one of his thugs take care of the matter in whatever manner they wanted. No questions asked.

Not anymore.

Now, he'd do it himself and enjoy every second of it. She deserved to die for giving his name to the authorities. Before she opened her big trap, they'd had no reason to link him and Kassidy together.

Dale tossed the FBI agent's business card in the trash and left his condo.

Once he got what he needed from the spoiled bitch, he'd make her pay, but perhaps not as much as her stepsister.

Yeah, Kassidy would suffer a hell of a lot more than Becca. Because of her double-cross, he was on the verge of losing out on millions while at the same time dishing out money to a thug like Zane. Not to mention, because she'd been unable to keep her mouth shut, her stepsister had known about their involvement and shared it with the damn Feds.

He entered the coffee shop and ordered. Despite the time, the place was packed, and he grabbed one of the last empty tables. For both their sakes, Zane better have news tonight. So help him, if Zane didn't get him what he wanted, he'd do everything in his power to bring the man and his organization down for good.

"Do you have my package?" Dale asked, the noise in the shop so loud tonight he covered his other ear to better hear Zane's response.

"Out for pickup."

"You're sure?" Zane had promised he'd have her already. Instead of delivering Becca, he kept giving Dale excuses.

"Been tracking her every move. I know exactly where she is. And I know where my guys are. We'll deliver her to you soon." Zane sounded a cocky as ever. "Have my payment."

"Half tonight," Dale snapped out. They'd already settled on the terms, and he wasn't open to renegotiating. "You get the other half when you bring me the second one." Dale ended the call and reached for his sandwich.

Shit. Dale's gaze hit the cell phone he'd put down before he got the sandwich off the table. He'd used the wrong phone. How the hell had he made such a mistake? Until now he'd been so careful. He'd only contacted Zane using the burner phone he'd purchased for that specific purpose, and he never made a call to him from his condo.

Tonight he'd screwed up, and he put the blame squarely on Becca André's shoulders. If not for her, the FBI wouldn't have made their visit and he wouldn't be preoccupied. No, his mind would still be focused on the end goal rather than revenge.

A single phone call to the guy isn't enough to prove anything, he reminded himself, and then bit into his sandwich. He had a long night to look forward to and didn't want something as simple as hunger getting in his way.

TWENTY

BECCA DRAINED another cup of the high-octane coffee. In order to drink it, she'd added so much cream and sugar that she'd probably ingested enough calories to equal three king-sized candy bars. She wasn't worried about it. Not tonight anyway. And at least drinking the stuff gave her something to do besides pace around HRT's kitchen or stare at the walls. She eyed the pot and considered pouring a fourth cup.

Better not. She already had the jitters, and another dose of caffeine might make them a semipermanent condition. Instead, she tossed the paper cup in the trash and selected a bottle of flavored water from the fridge.

Resuming her spot at the table, Becca wondered if someone would come in soon with an update. They'd returned to Elite Force hours ago, or at least it seemed like hours. Knowing her luck, only thirty or forty minutes had passed. Honestly, there was no way to tell. The kitchen she was sitting in had no windows, and no one had ever bothered to set the clock on the microwave. She assumed her cell phone was still wherever Connor had left it earlier, and she hadn't thought to ask him for it before he deposited her in here and walked away. Before they left the cabin, Connor had retrieved their personal belongings, including her watch, from the bedroom. Probably assuming she wouldn't need anything in the bag, he'd left it in the car rather than bring it inside the firm with them.

Through the doorway she watched two men exit the meeting room she'd sat in following the kidnapping attempt at the hospital, an event that felt like two lifetimes ago. Had it really been less than forty-eight hours ago? It seemed impossible, but she knew it was true.

The meeting room door opened again. Connor appeared in the hall, followed by Ax. They exchanged a few words before Ax walked away in one direction and Connor headed toward the kitchen. He wore a T-shirt, and there was a white bandage on his wound, yet she could still picture him standing there with blood dripping down his arm. It was a sight she'd never forget.

When he'd opened the closet door and she'd seen the blood, her heart had stopped. In that moment, she'd realized the truth. She wasn't falling in love with him. She was already there. The realization had quickly been followed by the thought that he might die because he'd been protecting her.

Even his verbal reassurance that the wound wasn't serious hadn't helped. Only after he'd wiped the blood away, allowing her to see he only had a gash and not an actual bullet hole through his arm, had her heart returned to a more normal beat.

"I don't have a lot of time, but I wanted to give you an update before I left," Connor explained, grabbing a coffee and joining her at the table. "Kassidy has been located."

He drank half the cup while she processed the four words. "As in you know where she is for certain, or HRT physically has her?"

"HRT was part of the team that went in, but the FBI has her in custody." He leaned toward her and placed a hand on her shoulder. "I wish I could give you more details, but I can't until I get the okay from Ax."

Details would be nice, but she understood. "Is she okay?"

Regardless of what Kassidy had or hadn't done, Becca hoped she remained unharmed.

"Yeah. She doesn't have a scratch on her."

All the other details would eventually come out, especially if she had stolen the research as everyone suspected. "Good. Has anyone told Robert?" Becca didn't need to speak to her stepfather to know the man was going crazy, not knowing whether Kassidy was okay or not.

"No idea. But if someone hasn't contacted him yet, they will." He drained his cup. "Thanks to cyber, we know where the bastard who's been after you is holed up."

Connor's mouth covered hers before she could ask if that had anything to do with why he didn't have a lot of time.

"It's almost over. But until I get back, you'll stay here."

"Where are you going?" She asked the question even though her mind already knew the answer. They'd managed to track down whoever had planted those little devices in her purse and briefcase, and he planned to go after them.

He met and held her gaze. "Exactly where you think, Becca."

The image of Connor's body motionless and covered in blood much like the intruders she'd seen tonight formed. Asking him not to go was pointless, regardless of her feelings. "Be careful."

Over Connor's shoulder, she spotted Maddie standing in the doorway. Becca didn't care if they had an audience or not. Closing her eyes, she took possession of his lips and focused all her attention on communicating her feelings to him.

"Save it, Romeo," a male voice she didn't recognize called into the room. "We're out of here."

She'd known at least one person was watching, but the comment from the newcomer made her blush anyway.

Connor pulled away and stood. "Be back soon. Mad Dog is going to keep you company." He moved away and paused at the doorway. "Keep her from thinking too much."

Yeah, not possible. Until he returned alive and unharmed, she'd be thinking about nothing but him.

"I'll do my best," Maddie answered before coming into the kitchen and picking up the cup Connor had left behind. "Man, I wish I was going with them." She tossed it into the trash can before pouring what was left in the coffeepot into a new cup.

Although it would mean being in danger, Becca shared the woman's sentiment. Connor hadn't even exited the building yet and already she was worrying. If she were with him, she wouldn't need to wait to find out if he was okay.

She watched Maddie—she just couldn't think of her as Mad Dog, no matter how many times she heard Connor call her that —get a fresh pot of coffee started.

"Did Ax or Connor ask you to babysit me?" A conversation wouldn't stop the thoughts going through her head, but it would help pass the time. Right now she couldn't do anything but pass time.

"Nah, I'm not allowed on any operations until I'm done with physical therapy." Finished at the counter, she joined Becca at the table. "I offered to keep you company while Connor's gone." She crossed her arms on the table. "And don't worry, he'll be back."

She wasn't worried if he'd be back; it was the state he'd be in when he came back that concerned her.

"Safely. So relax."

"Are mind reading abilities a prerequisite for a job here?" Becca inquired. More than once Connor had done the same thing to her.

Maddie smiled, and Becca again wondered why a woman would choose this type of career. "If such a thing existed, it might be," she replied. "Some people are easy to read. Whether you like it or not, you're one of them. But, like I said, there's no reason to worry. Connor and the team know what they're doing. He and everyone with him will return in one piece."

"How many are with him? Or can't you tell me?" On television, it was always two or three good guys going in after a gang of bad guys. She always guessed it didn't happen like that in real life. It would simply be too dangerous, but knowing for certain would go a long way right now.

"The team sent tonight consists of six and, trust me, they all know what they're doing." Maddie sounded confident. "Plus, they're not going in alone. Because it's believed this is tied to your stepsister, the FBI and the local police are involved as well."

"And they have the element of surprise," Becca added. At least she hoped they had surprise on their side. If whoever planted those devices knew the good guys were coming, they might be able to overtake Connor and whoever was with him.

Maddie nodded as she sipped her drink. "Yep. So you can stop worrying. Tomorrow at this time, the two of you will be naked, and you'll be showing Connor how much you love him. In the meantime, how about a game of cards? Or chess if you play."

The woman was blunt and far too perceptive. No wonder she and Connor were friends as well as coworkers.

But how the hell had Maddie determined she loved Connor? The truth had only hit her tonight at the cabin.

"The kiss you gave him before he left told me everything I needed to know."

How does she do that? Becca knew mind reading only existed in the fictional world, but if she didn't know better, she'd think Maddie was truly able to do it.

"Don't worry, I won't say anything to him," she said. "You can tell him yourself when he comes back."

If Connor and the other members of HRT trusted Maddie with their lives, Becca trusted her to keep anything they said between them. "Thank you." She considered Maddie's two suggestions. "If you have a chess set around, I'm up for a game." Right now, she'd do almost anything to pass the time.

"I have an electronic version on my tablet. Be right back."

"I'm not going anywhere."

A game of chess could last hours. Becca prayed she wasn't sitting here that long.

HE'D WORKED with several government agencies in the past. With a few exceptions, FBI agents were better than their counterparts from other agencies or the local police. Regardless, Connor and the other members of HRT preferred to work alone.

Especially this time around.

He'd experienced fear before. But he'd never experienced it like he had tonight. If he hadn't been there, or if he hadn't been able to stop the three intruders, Becca would be at the mercy of the animal after her. Various scenarios of what could've been done to Becca had tormented him throughout the ride back to Elite Force.

So, unlike other operations, this one was personal.

When they got the radio signal, they approached the perimeter of the home. According to property records, the estate belonged to a Michael Zane Jefferson, known to the police as Zane. He'd faced various criminal charges over the years. Except for the time he'd done as a juvenile, he had never been convicted.

A light switched on in an upstairs room, and a man passed by the window. Soon after, a woman walked by. Evidently, Zane had female company for the evening. Connor hoped the woman upstairs with him was the dude's only houseguest.

Considering what the guy had been charged with in the past and what the cops suspected he dabbled in, it was possible he kept a few thugs on hand just in case.

Weapon in hand, Connor took up his assigned position and waited.

He watched a member of the FBI SWAT team breach the door with the battering ram. The moment it was open, Connor moved into the house, his teammate Ryan right behind him as well as several FBI agents.

Not a soul bothered them.

He reached the second floor, expecting gunfire to erupt at any moment. Men like Zane didn't usually go quietly.

None came.

The house remained silent.

With his finger mere inches from the trigger, he moved down the hallway. The light had come from a room at the back of the house.

Connor turned a corner as a door opened. Light from inside flooded the hall, and a man stepped out. Fully dressed, he stood with his arms relaxed by his sides, palms facing out and an all-too-smug expression on his face. Despite the lack of any visible weapon, Connor kept his gun pointed in Zane's direction.

"FBI! Stay where you are, with your hands up!" the FBI agent closest to Connor shouted as he and another agent approached Zane with their weapons drawn.

He waited for the jerk to reach for a gun or make a run for it. Instead, he stood there as if having several armed men storm his house was an everyday occurrence.

"People usually knock before they enter someone's home. Or didn't they teach you that at Quantico?" Zane said.

The guy's got balls. Connor had gone in the house expecting either a firefight or an escape attempt. He hadn't expected to hear the man complaining because the authorities had come in to arrest him and failed to knock first.

"Michael Jefferson, you're under arrest," the tallest of the agents said, moving closer so he could slip handcuffs on him. "You have the—"

Zane cut the agent off before he got any further with the Miranda warning. "Under arrest for what?"

Unsurprisingly, his expression didn't change as the agent cuffed his hands behind his back and then searched him for any hidden weapons.

"Your role in the attempted kidnapping of Becca André," the agent answered.

"You have the right—" He started the Miranda warning over, but again Zane interrupted him.

"And when did this attempted kidnapping happen?"

The agent looked as baffled as Connor, but he answered. "Thursday night outside Washington General, and then again last night."

Zane shook his head. "I've been on vacation. We got back late last night." He tilted his head toward the room he'd exited. "Molly was with me. Feel free to speak with her or anyone at my home on Cape Hatteras where we stayed."

The agent acted as if the man hadn't opened his mouth and again reminded him he had the right to remain silent as the two agents who'd gone in the bedroom escorted Zane's company from the room.

Connor watched Zane be led away, the same smug expression still on his face. Damn, he'd love to be there when the guy learned what evidence they had against him. Because Zane wouldn't be smiling then. And no story his girlfriend or his employees gave would help him.

"That was fucking bizarre," Ryan said, holstering his gun. "How did a genius scientist from a top laboratory get mixed up with him?"

He'd been wondering that, as well as a few other things since getting Zane's dossier. Nothing in the man's criminal past indicated he'd have the contacts necessary for doing anything with the research Kassidy stole. Even if he did have the connections, how had Kassidy met the guy? A woman who dated congressmen and wealthy businessmen wouldn't get involved with a thug like Zane.

"Don't know," Connor admitted.

There was another piece missing. Or, rather, a third party missing. Eventually, the answers would come out, but this morning he had other matters to see to. Becca needed to know they'd gotten the man after her. And he planned to be the one to tell her.

STOPPING AT THE KITCHEN DOORWAY, he expected Becca to be sitting there. She wasn't. Only Mad Dog remained inside the room. She had her feet propped up on a chair and a tablet in her hands.

"Where is she?" he demanded.

Ax wouldn't let her wander around the floor alone, but she was free to leave the building at any time. If Ax had passed along that Zane was in custody, she might have gone home.

Mad Dog looked up from her tablet. "Nice to see you too. Things go smoothly?"

"Almost too smoothly." He'd spent the drive back thinking about the guy's reaction. Considering the charges facing him, Zane had been too relaxed. Connor didn't know what card the guy had to play, but he had one. "I thought you were keeping Becca company until I got back. Where is she?"

"Don't get your panties in a knot. Becca is fine. She fell asleep sitting here, and in case you didn't know, your girlfriend snores."

"And you put her where?"

"I got one of the cots cyber keeps on hand. Ax let me put it in the meeting room. She's in there, sleeping like a baby and dreaming about you."

More like dreaming about the events of the past forty-eight hours. She'd been having nightmares already. The shooting at the cabin wasn't going to help.

"Thanks for staying with her." He turned to leave.

"One of the men from the cabin made it through surgery."

One had been gone before the paramedics arrived. Despite their efforts, he'd expected the other two to be dead before they reached a hospital. "Good."

Given the right incentive from the district attorney, the punk might be willing to provide testimony that could be used against Zane.

He passed Ax's office. Later he'd check in with him. First, he had something much more important to do.

Connor didn't knock on the meeting room door before walking inside. Since it wasn't uncommon for employees in cyber to pull all-nighters when working on a case, the department kept cots on hand so they could rest. Tonight, one was pushed up against a wall and all the lights in the room were off.

Compared to the king-sized bed in Becca's home, the cot was about as comfortable as a hardwood floor. This morning it at least gave her a place to rest. He should've gotten one for her before he left, but his mind had been on other matters.

Sitting on the edge, he ran his fingers through her messy hair. Despite the less- than-ideal sleeping conditions, she looked content. More importantly, she was safe.

Back at the estate, he'd wanted to pull Zane into a room and show the asshole what happened when someone threatened the woman he loved. And he did love her.

He hadn't been looking for it or expecting it, but denying it was pointless.

In hindsight, maybe falling in love with Becca had been inevitable. She'd been the first and only woman he'd ever wanted to be with because he enjoyed her company, rather than because he was looking for physical pleasure.

She loved him too. He didn't need her to say the words. Her actions gave her away.

Becca moved onto her back and threw out an arm, her hand smacking into the gun still holstered at his waist. "Ouch." She opened her eyes and then bolted upright. "Good, you're back." Her gaze swept over him. "You look okay. Are you?"

"Fine."

"You're not just telling me that, are you, Connor? Because, so help me, if you are…."

Except for the occasional inquiry from his sister, no one ever questioned his well-being, let alone worried he might be injured. Becca's concern at the cabin and again this morning was only further evidence she loved him.

"When we get out of here, you can give me a thorough physical examination." He kissed her, because not doing so was impossible. Leaning into her, he pushed her back down on the cot.

How likely was it someone would walk in, looking for him? Mad Dog wouldn't bother them. However, Ax knew he was back and expected him to check in along with the rest of the team. He might not come searching for him right away.

Leaving her mouth, he moved his lips down her neck and gently tugged the collar of her shirt down.

Pounding on the door interrupted his mouth's pleasant trip south. "My office," Ax said, opening the door. "We're waiting for you."

Resting his forehead against Becca's chest, he swore.

"Heard you, Anderson," Ax called before walking away and leaving the door open.

Sitting up, he pulled Becca back into an upright position and fixed her shirt. "Be back soon. Get some more rest."

She grabbed his hand before he could stand. "Is it really over?"

"Kassidy and Zane are in custody, and both will be spending time behind bars. You're safe."

The distress on her face disappeared, and he could see the weight lift off her shoulders.

He gave her hand a quick squeeze and tried to stand again. "The sooner I go, the sooner I'll be back. Then we can split, and I can get back to what I was doing before Ax interrupted us."

TWENTY-ONE

AFTER POURING batter onto the Belgian waffle iron, Becca lowered the top and turned her attention to her laptop. Threat gone or not, the nightmares continued. Rather than disturb Connor this morning, she came downstairs to start breakfast after waking up from the most recent one. Eventually they would stop.

She hoped.

She hadn't had a decent night's sleep since before the break-in.

Opening her preferred internet browser, she typed in the address for her favorite news site. As expected, articles pertaining to Kassidy's arrest had been everywhere for the past few days. A story about a top scientist stealing research intended for military use was just too good for the press to ignore. The media would keep running articles until they got every dime they could from the story too.

Becca now had a better understanding of what Connor and his family must have gone through following the arrest and prosecution of his father. And each time she saw her stepsister's picture on a news site, she thought of Robert.

She'd talked to both her stepfather and mom following

Kassidy's arrest. He'd been in complete denial despite the evidence against Kassidy, evidence that included the hard drive with all the research data she hadn't yet sold to her buyer. Perhaps in his shoes she'd be in denial at first too. No parent wanted to believe his or her child would break the law and end up in prison.

She hadn't spoken to him again, but according to Mom, he'd since accepted the truth and hired a fantastic defense attorney for Kassidy. Not that even the best lawyer in the world would be able to keep her stepsister from serving time.

When the news site opened, she reached toward the touch pad, prepared to scroll past the articles about Kassidy and see what else was happening in the world. The first headline on the screen kept her fingers motionless.

Federal Authorities Arrest Congressman Dale Fuller.

The arrest of a congressman wasn't an everyday occurrence.

Becca scanned the article under the headline. Her eyes stopped when they passed over the name Kassidy Buchanan, and she reread the sentence.

She'd thought nothing else about Kassidy's arrest would surprise her. She'd been wrong.

Dale Fuller and Kassidy had been working together. *Unbelievable.*

Hoping the article would share the role the congressman had played in Kassidy's plot, she read the next paragraph.

Kidnapping for hire—the words jumped out from the long list of charges against the Virginia congressman.

Scrolling down, she continued reading, oblivious to everything else.

Beep! Beep! The smoke detector on the ceiling erupted, disturbing the quiet. Jumping up, Becca grabbed a dishtowel and waved it near the device until the offending sound stopped.

Then she went to check the damage.

"Crap." An overcooked waffle greeted her when she opened

the lid. Not even a gallon of maple syrup and strawberries would make it edible. She'd have to start a new one.

Removing it from the iron, she set it on a plate and reached for the mixing bowl.

"Maybe we should go out for breakfast." Coming up behind her, Connor kissed her neck and settled his hands on her waist. Despite the threat being gone, he'd stayed with her every night since the kidnapping attempt at the hospital.

Stupid smoke detector. She'd wanted to surprise him with breakfast in bed. "No need. I was reading the news and got distracted. I'll keep a closer eye on them this time." After pouring more batter into the machine, she closed the cover and turned. "Sorry I woke you. There's coffee if you want some, and I have some bacon in the oven."

"You didn't. The call from Ax did. When the smoke alarm went off, I was on my way down. Bacon in the oven?" He brushed his lips across hers before going for coffee.

"Trust me on this. It tastes so much better if you cook it under the broiler."

"Whatever you say." He took a seat at the kitchen island. "Anything interesting going on in the world this morning?"

"Interesting is one word you could use to describe today's breaking story." She took a sip of coffee before continuing. "Authorities have evidence connecting Kassidy, Michael Jefferson, and Congressman Dale Fuller. Fuller's been arrested, and he's facing a long list of charges. The article is still up on my computer if you want to read it."

The green light on the waffle iron went on, indicating the breakfast treat was ready. Before another waffle turned into an inedible piece of charcoal, she removed it and then covered it with fresh sliced strawberries.

"No need. I already know. Ax told me. It was part of why he called. Surprised the hell out of me too." He accepted the plate she handed him and smiled. "This looks amazing. Thank you." He didn't bother to add any maple syrup before he dug in. "I figured there was another party involved. Never expected it to be a congressman. Not even after you gave us the guy's name." He cut another large segment off his waffle. "Both Kassidy and Zane implicated Fuller and turned over evidence against him."

She carried her waffle and the bacon over to the island. "Do you think they did it in exchange for lesser charges or something?" Right or wrong, it was a common practice in the judicial system.

Snagging a few slices of bacon, he shrugged. "Possibly, or they gave him up because if they were going to prison they wanted his ass there too. Ax didn't say, and I didn't ask."

She wanted the congressman to pay for whatever role he'd played. At the same time, Becca hated the idea of Kassidy and Zane getting off easy after all the suffering they'd caused. "I know it sounds terrible because she's family and everything, but I hope Kassidy stays locked up for a long time."

He paused with a strip of bacon almost to his lips. "No, it doesn't." Lines of concentration deepened along his brows and under his eyes. "When my father was arrested, I refused to believe it at first. After all the facts came out and I learned the full extent of what he'd done, I hoped he'd rot in jail. And I haven't talked to him since." Reaching over, he covered her hand with his. "Anyone in your position would be thinking the same thing." He gave her hand a little squeeze. "Considering the danger she put you in, I hope she never gets out. You don't want to know what I'd like to see happen to the congressman and Zane."

He'd risked his life to protect her. Somehow saying thank you didn't seem sufficient, but she'd tell him anyway. "I should've said this sooner, but thank you. If not for you, I'd be who knows where."

"No thanks needed. I protect the people I love. I'd do whatever I had to do to keep you safe."

She'd known he'd cared about her, but hadn't expected him to drop the L-word over waffles and bacon. Since he'd said it, she couldn't think of a good reason not to admit the truth herself. "I love you too."

She expected some sign of surprise. Instead he said, "I know." Then he reached for his bacon again.

Was he giving her hard time, or had he known before she opened her mouth? "Really? And how did you figure it out?"

"Easy." He shrugged, the gesture annoying her just the slightest bit. "You don't hide your thoughts or feelings well."

So, more or less, he was telling her she was easy to read too. She'd never thought of herself that way. Maybe she should start, and at the same time work on keeping her emotions under wraps.

"It's not a bad trait," he added. "Just means you'd never be able to deceive people the same way Kassidy or my father did. And you probably have a terrible poker face. I recommend staying away from Vegas."

When he put it that way, it didn't sound like much of a flaw. Placing both elbows on the granite countertop, she leaned forward. "And what am I thinking now?"

The smile he gave her sent her pulse racing and warmed her across the space separating them. "You want to take me upstairs and show me how much you love me."

He's not wrong.

───────

YEAH, he'd known she loved him before she said anything. But he hadn't realized how much hearing the words would affect him. When she told him, it'd been like receiving a shot of adrenaline. And he was still riding the high.

Next to him, Becca moved, propping herself up on her elbow. "Life's crazy, isn't it?" Slipping her hand onto his chest, she continued. "When we ran into each other at the café, I hadn't thought much about you in years. And I had no idea what to expect before our picnic."

"Not me." He folded an arm under his head and readjusted

the sheet near his waist. "I thought it'd be a one-and-done kind of day. We'd catch up then both go back to our own worlds."

She frowned, and the fingers brushing against his skin stopped. "Before you say it, I know your thoughts from back then shouldn't bother me. But they do."

His experience in the relationship department was limited. Still, even he knew telling the person you loved and who at the moment happened to be lying next to you naked that you'd always hooked up with women simply to get laid was a bad idea. So he softened the truth the best he could. "Becca, it had nothing to do with you. I've never wanted or looked for the type of relationships you've had."

She stared at him as if he'd grown a third arm. "Seriously? Never?"

"No. I liked being able to do what I wanted without considering or worrying about anyone else."

"And now?"

You knew that one was coming. "I've got you."

EPILOGUE

FOUR MONTHS later

JUGGLING her briefcase and the takeout bags from Cooper's Smokehouse, she slid her key into the lock. *Put up the wreath,* she reminded herself again at the sight of the bare door. If she waited much longer to do it, the holidays would be over and gone.

She'd switched the interior lights on before getting out of her car, so rather than walking into a dark, empty house, she simply walked into an empty one. Thankfully, it wouldn't be empty for long. After landing at the airport, Connor had sent her a text message, letting her know he'd be over once he had his luggage. Since the message had come over an hour ago, he should be here soon.

It'd been over a week since she saw him. One incredibly long week, and she hoped Elite Force didn't send him away again anytime soon. Especially with the holidays around the corner.

She hadn't asked him yet, but she hoped he'd come up to Connecticut with her for Christmas this month. Considering the way he'd avoided the area over the years, she wasn't certain what kind of response she'd get when she brought up the subject. She planned on asking anyway. It wasn't the only thing she intended to ask him tonight.

When he wasn't away on an assignment, he spent more time at her house than his. To the point it didn't make sense for him to own a place.

While his response to her first question remained a mystery, she was confident he'd agree to move in when she asked him her second.

Or perhaps I'll ask him to move in first. Either way, she planned on showing him how much she'd missed him over the past several days.

As much as she hated when he left for days on end, she thoroughly enjoyed their reunions when he returned.

Her stomach growled as she set down the takeout bags. She'd missed lunch, and until now, the lack of food in hours hadn't bothered her. However, her brain and stomach had taken notice of the delicious aromas filling the kitchen and decided a vocal protest was in order.

Maybe one piece of corn bread while I wait. She selected the smallest slice from the container and bit into the still-warm bread. The techno song she'd set as Graham's ringtone recently erupted from her cell phone as she took a second bite.

Although never polite to answer with a mouthful of food, considering it was only her brother, she did it anyway. "Hey, Graham."

"Have you seen the news?"

Not exactly the greeting she expected, especially from her always-polite brother. "Not today. And I only got home a few moments ago." Even if she'd been home for hours, she probably wouldn't have seen the news. It was Friday. She wanted to put the rest of the world aside until Monday morning. "What happened?"

Had there been something in the news about Kassidy again?

Thankfully, over the past several weeks the story had died down, and the media had found other topics to report.

"Dale Fuller was attacked in prison."

Even with round-the-clock prison guards, inmates attacked each other. And sometimes those attacks had deadly outcomes. "Seriously? When? What happened?"

"According to the news, it happened around noon today. He was taken to the hospital with life-threatening injuries."

Good. Guilt smacked her hard.

"And it couldn't have happened to a better guy," Graham added before she spoke again.

The fact that he shared her sentiments helped ease her conscience. "It sounds really terrible, but I have to agree."

Across the house, she heard the door open. *Finally.* She'd given Connor a key two months ago. "I need to go, Connor's here, but thanks for letting me know. I'll call you soon."

"Say hi to him for me. Are we still on for dinner next week?"

Connor entered the room and any guilt remaining vanished. "Yep. See you then."

She barely got the phone down before he claimed her lips, ravishing her mouth and setting off tiny denotations throughout her body.

Pulling away, Connor removed the sandalwood hairpins holding her bun in place then ran his fingers through her hair. "I missed you."

"Believe me, the feeling is mutual. And I don't plan on letting you leave this house again until Monday." She moved from his embrace and kicked off her shoes. "Have a seat and I'll grab some beers so we can eat. There should be paper plates in the bag. I don't know about you, but I'm starving."

"Cooper's tonight?"

"Yep." She set the drinks down while Connor removed the individual dishes from the large bag. "When you walked in, I was talking to Graham. He called to tell me former Congressman Fuller was attacked in prison."

"YEAH, I HEARD." He'd seen it on the news while waiting for his connecting flight to board, a flight that had been delayed by three hours, turning his layover into a five-hour headache. Later Ax called to give him the news. "I'm not surprised."

Or disappointed. The guy had tried to kidnap Becca. In his opinion, prison time was too good for him.

"Guess I'm the only one who didn't."

"I was waiting for my flight out of Logan when it hit the news." He grabbed the container of pulled pork and piled it onto his plate. He hadn't had a decent meal all day. "Ax let me know too."

"Did he know the man's status?"

"When he called, Fuller had made it through surgery and had been moved to the intensive care unit. But that was right before I left Boston, so it might have changed." The devil in him hoped it had, and not for the better.

Becca looked torn by his answer, and he didn't need to ask to know why. "I guess that's good." She sipped her beer and then went back to eating.

She didn't say another word for several minutes. He kept his trap shut too. He'd been with her long enough to recognize the signs. She was working through something in her head. When she was ready, she'd share. Until then he'd eat dinner, drink his beer, and enjoy her company.

"I want to talk to you about a couple things." Becca set her fork down and focused on him.

Considering the seriousness of her expression and tone, he did the same. "Go for it."

"Move in with me." She slipped her hand over his, the slight physical contact amping up the sexual hunger already prowling through his body. "I love you and hate it when you're not around. You spend more time here than at your place anyway."

He'd considered asking her to move in with him but had

decided against it. The commute from his place to her office every day would suck.

"You don't have to give me an answer tonight. Whenever you're ready."

"Nothing to think about. Consider me your new roommate."

The smile she sent him went straight to his heart.

"What else do you want to talk about?"

His question dimmed her smile. *Bad sign.*

"Both my parents have holiday parties planned this month. Mom and Robert have theirs scheduled for the nineteenth. Dad and Cecilia planned theirs for the twenty-third. I usually go to both."

Ever since he spotted the first decorated Christmas tree, he'd been thinking about the upcoming holiday and gift ideas. It'd been years since he did any real celebrating or shopping. He hadn't had anyone in his life he wanted to buy a present for until now.

The tip of her tongue ran across her bottom lip, distracting him from thoughts of holiday presents and reminding him of the ways she often pleasured him with her tongue. Once they finished this conversation, they were done talking for a while.

"I know you don't go back to Greenwich much, Connor."

Much? More like ever. The closest he'd gotten in years was Boston, and it was over 180 miles away from his hometown.

"And I understand why. Really, I do. But I'd love it if you came up with me. Even if it's only for one of the parties. We don't have to stay through Christmas."

A night having screws jammed under his fingernails held more appeal than a party surrounded by the people he'd cut from his life, but he had more than himself to consider these days. Becca wasn't talking about just any holiday parties. These were ones her family was throwing.

"I don't remember the last time I went anywhere near town." If he told her he couldn't take the time off to travel, it would get him out of attending. In the months they'd been together, he'd never lied to her. He wouldn't start tonight. "There's not a person there I want to associate with."

She sighed and slumped back against her chair. "I assumed you'd say no. It's okay. I get it. I'll go alone."

"Back the ship up. If I never went back, I'd be fine. And if anyone else asked me to visit, hell, even if it was my mother, I'd say no. But you're not anyone. If you want me to go, then I'll go. I'll talk to Ax about taking time off."

"Really?"

"There's not a single thing I wouldn't do for you." The smile his words earned him was worth the unpleasant visit staring him in the face. "Now, let's finish eating so you can show me how appreciative you are." He winked and reached for his fork again.

Pushing her chair back, Becca came around the table and grabbed his hand. "Why wait?"

No further invitation was required.

The End

ABOUT THE AUTHOR

USA Today Best Selling author, Christina Tetreault started writing at the age of 10 on her grandmother's manual typewriter and never stopped. Born and raised in Lincoln, Rhode Island, she has lived in four of the six New England states since getting married in 2001. Today, she lives in New Hampshire with her husband, three daughters and two dogs. When she's am not driving her daughters around to their various activities or chasing around the dogs, she is working on a story or reading a romance novel. Currently, she has three series out, The Sherbrookes of Newport, Love on The North Shore and Elite Force Security. You can visit her website http://www.christinatetreault.com or follow her on Facebook to learn more about her characters and to track her progress on current writing projects.

OTHER BOOKS BY CHRISTINA

The Sherbrookes of Newport Series

*Loving The Billionaire, a novella

*The Teacher's Billionaire

*The Billionaire Playboy

*The Billionaire Princess

*The Billionaire's Best Friend

*Redeeming The Billionaire

*More Than A Billionaire

*Protecting The Billionaire

*Bidding On The Billionaire

*Falling For The Billionaire

*The Billionaire Next Door

*The Billionaire's Homecoming

*The Billionaire's Heart, coming soon

Love On The North Shore Series

+The Courage To Love

+Hometown Love

+The Playboy Next Door

+In His Kiss

+A Promise To Keep

Elite Force Security

^Born To Protect